A CLUTCH OF VIPERS

Books by Jack S. Scott

A Clutch of Vipers
The Shallow Grave
The Bastard's Name Was Bristow
The Poor Old Lady's Dead

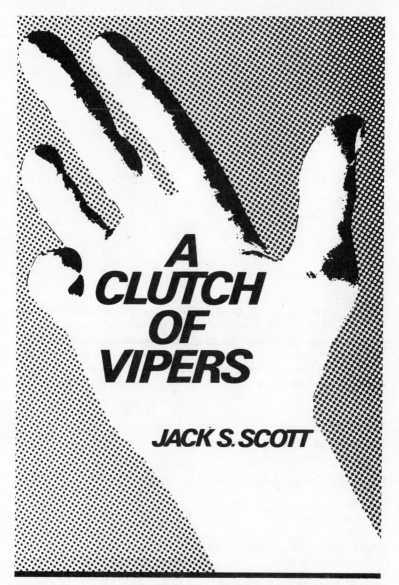

A CLUTCH OF VIPERS

JACK S. SCOTT

HARPER & ROW, PUBLISHERS
NEW YORK, HAGERSTOWN, SAN FRANCISCO, LONDON

A HARPER NOVEL OF SUSPENSE

FIRST U.S. EDITION

Designed by Sidney Feinberg

Library of Congress Cataloging in Publication Data

Scott, Jack S.
  A clutch of vipers.
  I. Title.
PZ4.S4264CL   1979   [PS3569.C633]   813'.5'4
  ISBN 0-06-014008-9   78-22451

79 80 81 82 83 10 9 8 7 6 5 4 3 2 1

A CLUTCH OF VIPERS

1

One small coincidence sparked the matter: Detective Sergeant Alfred Stanley Rosher and Mad Frankie Daly chose the same July day to insert classified advertisements into the town evening paper. And here is how that came about: Mad Frankie was setting up a job, and Sergeant Rosher needed domestic help. Big oaks from little acorns grow. Three deaths and a deal of anguish, out of this one.

Mad Frankie was planning big tickle. This is why he sat in his luxury apartment on a hot and clammy evening scanning a copy of *The Evening Courier*. Not every cry in the personal column on the lines of ADA COME HOME tells a story of family tears and tribulation. For example, take Frankie's, so worded as to summon certain men selected for this enterprise and to warn others to stay clear, they being judged superfluous.

Just under the "Used Cars" column he found it, and checked the wording. Satisfied, he was about to pass on to the racing page when he noticed the insertion immediately beneath. He said to Jokey Fenton, present with him in the Indian-carpeted, beautifully furnished room (he paid a man in cerise corduroy to do it for him, expense no object after a highly successful brandy-and-baccy hijack):

"Rosher. Clapper's Mount. Would that be the Rosher?"

The words came from his handsome lips in a rich brogue. He raised the beautiful Irish eyes that smiled even as he corrected an overambitious rival or a naughty minion by thumping his spine with a pickax handle, or booted his face to pulp down a dark alley with the loom of unsmiling henchmen standing around. Mad Frankie liked to have a privileged few look on at the application of discipline, so that they could tell their friends. Generally speaking, they enjoyed it, too.

"Rosher?" said Jokey Fenton. "Dunno. He lives up that way somewhere. Why?" He was cleaning his nails with the knife carried usually in his sock, or in a side pocket more handy for fast-draw work. This is a thing criminals often do. They toy with brass knuckles and knives and the other portable tools of their trade. Particularly given to fiddling with things are villains physically on the small side. Like Jokey Fenton, who was quite small and very deadly.

Frankie quoted, in the sweet voice that tickled ripples into the soft underbelly of women who came, usually, to rue the day. "Wanted, housekeeper. Able to cook. Rosher, 'Holmleigh,' Clapper's Mount. Tel: 1392."

"Bastard," said Jokey. Not with particular vehemence, but because in villainous circles reference to any given policeman draws automatic response. Bastard is a standard term, not necessarily implying illicit sexual connection between the parents of the copper under scrutiny; any more than does the same term used by coppers, talking about a villain.

Mad Frankie reached for the telephone book, and riffled through to the R's. "Yes," he said, when he had checked. "Yes—it's him."

"Bastard," said Jokey, latest in the long line of men on both sides of the law who had been calling Rosher it for many, many years.

Frankie sat for a while, thinking in the sumptuous leather

armchair placed conveniently near to the bright yellow telephone, so that he did not have to move more than an arm to answer it. Six elegant, curly-dark feet of him, to go with the brogue and the smiling blue eyes. No wonder women tickled for him. Jokey, who lived close by him to guard that muscular body— well able to take care of itself, but a competent knife man is extremely useful, for watching the back—finished his nail paring and replaced the knife carefully in his sock. An antique carriage clock chimed softly, vibrating conditioned air tinted with aftershave and masculine deodorants. In matters of personal body care Frankie and his immediate associates could not be faulted; he was fussy about things like that. At length he reached a cashmere-clad arm; took the telephone into his lap, saying as he lifted the receiver and began to dial:

"Now here's a thing. We can use this—we can sew him up, if we play it right."

"What for?" asked Jokey, who like any prudent villain preferred to let sleeping police lie. Stir 'em up, you never know where it will end. "Sewed up already, ain't he? No bother, since they bust him down."

He said it with a grin. It was still a source of happiness among the bent fraternity, the busting down of a once formidable Detective Inspector to Detective Sergeant, virtually deskbound in a CID room, co-relating paperwork to do with stolen bicycles and allotment shed burglaries.

"The fun of it, boyo," said Frankie, and his vivid eyes sparkled; as always, when his sense of humor began to tick. He finished dialing and sat with the receiver burrp-burring in his ear.

"Leave the bastards alone, is what I say," Jokey told him. The grin was gone. He recognized the onset of Irish whimsy.

"Ah, but you have no *joie de vivre*," his boss said; and spoke richly into the phone, smile spread easily between eyes and voice as a little tin voice answered from the horrible city of Birmingham.

"Hallo, who's speaking? Margaret, hallo, me darling. Frankie." Broad smile, while the tin voice squeaked. "Is it that distinctive, then? You never know what you sound like to other people, do you? Listen, darling, you're the very girl I wanted. Remember Rosher?"

Now the voice positively squawked. Listening, Jokey thought uneasily: Leave the bastards alone, I say. We got too many things going, the job coming up and all. Frankie spoke again. "Yes—yes, I know, me darling. That's why I thought of you. How'd you like to help me set him up? Yes. Yes. No, I haven't worked the details out yet; the thought just came to me, something I saw in the paper. You and me together, I think we can finish him off. Interested? All right, my love. I'll ring you back. No need to hover over the phone. I have to give the matter a little thought. No hurry."

The job, thought Jokey. *That's* what you'd better keep thinking about, not farting about on the side.

"Right. Good girl. How's business?" He listened, smiling, to a brief reply. Brothels do not discuss such matters in detail over the phone, even to the man with the controlling interest. He would raise merry Cain if they did. So the answer was brief. "Good," said Frankie. "Good. I'll ring you back, then. Look after yourself, my darling." And he put the phone down. Reaching out the cashmere-covered arm again to replace the pretty thing on its elegant table, he spoke to Jokey. "D'ye know who that was?"

"Princess Margaret. Inviting you to a dirty fortnight in Benidorm, all found." Men called him Jokey—waggish variation on the theme of Joe—as tribute to his lightning wit. He was at his best when a friend appeared with the fresh shiv marks sewn up all over his face. No smile on him now. But then, there seldom was.

Frankie acknowledged the jest with a slight wrinkling at the corners of those eyes, a stretching of the sculptured lips. "Margaret Brian," he said.

"What do you want her for?" Jokey asked. A small and cunning head he had, set narrowly on a thin and cunning body. Very pale skin, a whiter white than nightclub or prison pallor.

4

Many naturally vicious rogues have this skin, those who delight in torture and murder. Say this for Frankie: He used violence only as a business measure, having intelligence enough to know that he who lives and gets his kicks from sinking knives in the belly eventually winds up with a knife in the belly; so Jokey's opportunities for bloodletting were limited. But he had the skin for it.

"Mad for Nobby. Wasn't she? If anybody hates Rosher, there's the one. Swore she'd get him, didn't she?"

She did. Norman (Nobby) Brian, one-time associate of Frankie and a power in his own right, went up for twelve years. Rosher did that. To Margaret, his wife and crazy about him, he swore before, during, and after the trial, when she visited, that he never was near the bloody warehouse, never fired a gun when the copper came over the wall. How could he, when he wasn't even there? Rosher fixed him. Planted money. Fixed him. He was innocent. Innocent.

Well, perhaps he was. Of that particular crime. Rosher, be it admitted, was never too nice to manipulate, if he needed to; and for sure, Nobby was guilty of much that never homed to him—so much that he formed the arrogant and often fatal habit of sneering openly at the police. A silly habit, as wiser men could have told him, because you do that and the bastards will get you in the end. Rosher got Nobby, and Nobby knew he was got from the moment he was brought in for questioning, by the hard, triumphant look in Rosher's eye. This, of course, was when Old Blubbergut was a Detective Inspector, before the fall.

So Nobby swore he was innocent; and Margaret, in the way of loving women, believed him implicitly. And then Nobby was found dead in his cell, his jugular vein opened with a small piece of glass found on the floor beside him. Suicide, the coroner said; but it could have been done by one of the boys inside with him. Never a popular man, Nobby. Too arrogant. Had his quota of enemies.

It cut Margaret up badly. She swore a mighty oath. To get Rosher. To kill him, to see him squirm as he died.

Well, many people had similarly sworn. Nobody had managed it yet. It is a normal condition for coppers, to walk about with the threat of bloodcurdling vengeance hanging around them, screamed often from the dock by people going down, mostly proclaiming lily-white innocence. Surprisingly few die of it.

None of this background history had to be blocked in for Jokey's sake. He knew it all well enough; it came up still for occasional debate when villains relaxed with a jug or two in the places where they gather. There were men who swore the screws had done it, others imputed it to Charlie Withers, in at the time for armed robbery and a known hater of Nobby, who kept to himself too great a percentage of the proceeds from an enterprise in which they were concerned together. Likewise, it was no secret among the cognoscenti that Frankie had taken care of the widow by putting her in charge of one of his brothels, tucked away in a suburb of Birmingham. She did a good job, but never performed herself. Nor did Frankie ask her to, as a mark of respect for the dead. Knowing all this, then, Jokey merely said:

"So she said she'd get him. Hasn't done it yet, has she?"

"Ah, boyo," said Frankie, with that light still in his eyes, "but this could be her big chance. Yes. Yes, this could be her big chance."

He lapsed into smiling thought again, taking no notice whatsoever when Jokey expressed the opinion that they shouldn't start farting about, not now with this job coming up. After a while the smile spread to a near chuckle, and the arm went out to gather the phone, a well-tended finger dialed. This time a deeper tin voice answered, from west of Wolverhampton.

"Hallo," said Frankie. "Herbert? Hallo, me bucko—how are you? Good—good. Yes, fine. How's Ethel? Good. Listen now, Herbert. What I wanted to talk to you about: The kid you used in the last batch of photos—yes, the little blonde." The photos had involved a dildo, a divan, and a colored gentleman who appeared to squint. As many a man might, getting up to the things he was up to, clad only in his socks. "How old would she be? No—no—no trouble, I just wondered. Thirteen. Good. That's good. There might be a thing I'd like her to do for me. I'll ring you back. Give my love to Ethel." He hung up.

"What's the caper, then?" asked Jokey.

"A little idea's in my head," said his handsome boss. "Just a little thing, is all."

"You didn't ought to start farting about," Jokey said. "Not with this job coming up." He'd said it before, and not a blind bit of notice taken.

"The job's straightforward enough, bucko." Frankie was all smile, his eyes looking inward, watching the idea grow. "A man needs a little relaxation. A hobby, so to speak."

"You didn't ought to start farting about—." When Jokey nailed a phrase, he stayed loyally with it.

"Never let you down yet, have I?" A different gleam in Frankie's eye. He hated to have his actions queried. And this was true: The loyalties of men like Jokey are bought with results, and Frankie was a good leader, an intelligent operator with flashes of imaginative brilliance—he was Irish, wasn't he?—having a record that stood proud, encompassing some very good jobs indeed, and very little bird. Since he moved into the parish six years ago from Dublin, which became a little too hot, the small circle he gathered around him had prospered, and when one of them unfortunately went down, it was never for a job planned and executed by Frankie. Villains appreciate little things like that.

He himself had hardly been to prison since his wild Irish youth, and this in spite of the fact that three of his chief Dublin rivals had vanished, good Catholic lads like him, immediately after being seen drinking with him and the boys. But then, the bodies were never found. The Dublin cognoscenti and the Irish Constabulary both inclined to the belief that they now lay deep in a wild Irish bog. Only nobody knew where. Be the matter as it may, from then, wherever he moved he found a policeman, snub-nosed and with smiling eyes like his own. So he emigrated, seeking greater job opportunities; as millions of his compatriots have done through the spud-scented centuries.

Now he sat happily in his very nice flat, brewing the sort of mischief that appealed strongly to his Irish sense of humor; and Jokey said no more. Not much point—whatever argument was advanced, Frankie would go his own way. Out from the sock came the knife again, and the cunning-headed little man filled in with more nail-trimming the new silence while his chief sat thinking; until Frankie chuckled suddenly, and snapped his fingers, and reached once more for the phone. This time his dialing, by the normal miracle of modern electronics, brought him a voice from Bradford.

"Hallo," he said. "Mrs. Burt? How are you, my dear? Good. Good. Is Jimmy there? Frankie Daly. Thank you." He sat back for a moment; spoke again when the new, young voice came on the line. "Jimmy—how are you, my son? Good. Staying out of trouble? Good. Good. Listen—how do you fancy a little holiday? Yes—I might want you to do a job for me. Nothing very much—you'll enjoy it. Yes—yes—there'll be a few bob in it, of course there will. Have I ever asked you to work for me free? We'll discuss that later. Thing is, I've got this little idea. I'll ring you back. O.K.? Good. Watch how you go, now. And Jimmy—be a good lad—don't get yourself nicked between now and when I ring you." Laughing at some response from Bradford, he put the receiver into its cradle.

"Jimmy Burt?" said Jokey Fenton. "What do you want him for?" Right little bastard, Jimmy Burt. He'd make a name for himself one day, the juvenile courts left behind. For killing a copper, probably, with his lips curved angelically into his choirboy's smile. Jokey had worked with Jimmy's father once, on a pay-snatch job at Bradford. And a right bastard he'd been. Same angelic look about him, too. Except when he snarled.

"Part of me little hobby," Frankie told him, and began to dial again. Local call. This time he got straight through to the person whose ear he was seeking: Councillor Mrs. Bagster.

Detective Sergeant Rosher's reason for creating the advert that opened him up to the machinations of Mad Frankie Daly was as follows: He was broken in morale, battered in spirit, and after three months of it, fed to the brown teeth with trying to look after himself in the house from which his fat wife had decamped blubbering, going home to Mother. She'd waddled out of the door and out of his life in all her lachrymose avoirdupois, at the time of shattering aftermath to the disastrous affair involving a murder, a pub, and the landlord's too toothsome wife.

She went, poor creature, with all her carefully cherished illusions finally, irrevocably destroyed; because in his emotional agony he made it snarlingly clear that he didn't want her to stand by him, which is what she had intended to do; that he hated her, and had done through all the years since she transmogrified by food the slim and pretty girl he married, fattening her rapidly into the grotesque she now was, and had been for a long time.

Her going was the one bright spot in the black period that saw him, when he came out of hospital—Detective Inspector Rosher, two years from retirement and securely bumptious as a ranking policeman tends to be after many years of packing away villains to where they belong—bust down at the enquiry instigated by his fulminous Chief Constable to Detective Sergeant and lucky not to face a criminal assault charge explosive enough to set the press gobbling and to have blown him out of the force forthwith.

Three months ago she'd left him; and humiliated by his downgrading, tormented by the self-castigating inner turmoil that comes with enforced recognition of one's own stupidity, bumptious self-esteem shattered, not to have her red-eyed and blubberous around the house was, at first, a relief. Emotionally, since for many years she had not touched his emotions except with loathing, he had not missed her.

But after a while of going it alone—pigging it alone, as a disoriented and depressed man will, with no feminine check upon his domestic habits—he began to miss her apple pies and the sweet steam of steak and kidney puddings, served as soon as he came in amid tidy surroundings on clean plates. The baked bean upon toast is a delicacy that quickly palls, never mind what the television commercials say. So does the practice of eating out, especially in the class of restaurant falling within the compass of a Detective Sergeant's salary; more especially when the copper concerned is a man notoriously frugal. It comes hard, to pay for food; even when the saving is, in truth, very substantial. Because, my God, how his wife ate! But how she could cook!

Milk boiling over is what had finally goaded pen to paper. He'd had his Brekkie Shreddies in a bowl newly rinsed of whatever it had held before under the tap above a sink filled with dirty crockery; and he'd gone away to pick up the morning paper from the front-door mat.

It does not take long to pick up a paper from a mat, a few seconds only; but when he came back, the bloody milk was up and hissing again, adding white foam to gray grease and gravy stains working up by now to a crust on the cooker once kept whitely gleaming by a fat woman's art.

He must have had the gas much too high; because what smidgen of milk was left serviceable in the pan would hardly have moistened a lone cornflake, never mind a Brekkie Shreddie, which is a different matter entirely. Delicious with strawberries and cream, the manufacturer maintains. It well could be, bits of old flock mattress are delicious with strawberries and cream. In naked grittiness the Brekkie Shreddie is horrible; so Detective Sergeant Rosher turned the gas out, said fuck it (his very words), because he must needs go without breakfast, having forgotten again to buy eggs and the like; and in despair and sick fury, wrote out his advertisement at about the time when Frankie Daly, in much better order because he was never short of a woman (and anyway, flat-cleaning went with the lease) concocted his.

No doubt about it, the Sergeant badly needed a woman. Not sexually—sex it was that had destroyed him; and since the climacteric flare-up that fixated on the publican's well-endowed wife, he had been impotent. More than impotent—gut-churningly revolted by the very idea of sex.

The specific revulsion he had felt for long enough in relation to his fat wife spread out now to all the prettier, slimmer women he had lecherously enjoyed in fantasy, to compensate starvation. Suddenly, he saw them, painted skulls hanked with hair, where before he had seen softness of lips and smoothness of skin, life springing in that same hair and clear eyes in the molded desirable bone. Even his confessing, now, need for a woman in any capacity was a kind of capitulation. But somebody had to darn his socks, a hand more skilled than his must order the boiling of the milk.

Councillor Mrs. Bagster, when she answered the phone, felt the heart leap under her great, jutting, corset-controlled bust as the rich brogue spoke into her ear. "Annie?" it said. She hated to be called Annie. "Just the person I wanted a word with. How are you, dear?"

"Oh," she said. "It's—you."

"Frankie Daly. And how are you finding yourself? I liked your speech at the Education Committee meeting the other night. Just been reading about it in the *Courier*."

"Ah." All the nerves in her six-foot and bolster-built frame were jumping about, the blood leaping cold from her pounding heart. She added, because he had paused as if leaving space for her reply: "Thank you."

"Keep it up. They tell me you're a cert for mayor next year." Playful and bantering, the tone in the feared, beautiful voice. It went on: "Now, my love—what I'm ringing about. I want you to do a little thing for me. Just a little joke I've thought up. Have you seen this evening's *Courier*? No? Well—there's a classified ad—"

When he had outlined his idea, she said: "But—I can't. How can I—"

The voice broke in, playful as ever. "Och now, darling, of course you can. You're the big noise on all the charities, aren't you now? Get the local vicar in on it—say she's a bashed-up wife. Say you're acting for Shelter. Say what you like, but get

11

her in there. Oh, and there may be a couple of kids with her, I haven't decided yet. I'll ring you back later with all the details."

"But—" said Councillor Mrs. Bagster, "but—he may have engaged somebody—else—"

"Then it's up to you to blow them out, darling, isn't it? I leave it to you how you do it; if you take my advice, you'll call on the vicar."

"You're not—" she said; and paused to swallow against dryness in her throat. "You're not going to—rob him?"

Deprecatingly, playfully soothing, the voice protested: "No, no, no—don't be silly. What would he have that I'd want? A little policeman is all he is, entirely. A joke, darling—a little joke I have in my mind, that's all."

"I don't see why you want me to—" the councillor said.

Now the voice smoothed all the way down to urbane softness. "I want her in there, Annie. O.K.? I like my little jokes. Don't I?" Click, and the burring in her ear.

Jokey Fenton said, after the phone went down in the expensive flat: "I still don't reckon you ought to be frigging about. Not now. What do you reckon to get out of it, for Chrissake?"

"Fun, my buck," Frankie told him. "Relaxation. All work and no play."

"You can play when the bloody job's over."

"Ah, but you have to seize opportunity when it knocks. And it's knocking now. Think about it—get Maggie in there, she can plant whatever we give her. Get the kids in—there's no limit. We can sew him up tight."

"Oh, for Chrissake, he's bloody harmless. Down at the station, they call him 'the Bicycle King.' He's busted."

"Wasn't always harmless, was he now?" said Frankie, lightly. "A lot of good men he put away."

"Bastard," said Jokey, more viciously than before. He himself had been subjected more than once to the old, bombastic Rosher's hectoring, sneering style, brought in for questioning. Once, indeed, Rosher got him as far as the dock; but the charge failed to stick.

"So we owe them all something, don't we? He planted the

dope on Bert Harnet, didn't he? And he got Tommy Randal. Right? And Tommy was with me—you were with us—when Rosher said he was doing the jeweler's. And Nobby always swore he never went near that warehouse."

"Nobby'd swear anything," said Jokey.

"So would our little pal Rosher." Frankie never used foul language, in deference to the memory of the Holy Fathers who brought him up. Very unusual, among criminals. As among policemen. "So, now it's his turn. See how he enjoys it."

Soon after, they left for the out-of-town roadhouse where the boys would be gathering in response to the Annie-come-home advertisement. No serious planning, at this stage—not much planning necessary, the job was straightforward enough. With all his brothel, dope, and pornographic photo and film interests there was no real need for Frankie to pull any such job; but the kick of adrenaline is a drug in itself, and a chief is not a chief, least of all in his own eyes, unless he leads action from the front. Even the Mafia hierarchy need to display their power from time to time, lest the rank-and-file forget they possess it.

So he did as he always did. He stood dinner for the boys, he joined in the exuberant talk and laughter—they were excited by the prospect of working on one of his rich tickles—he picked up the tab for the drinks; and when they were gone, he sat on with Jokey at the table with his well-gratified belly crooning contentedly and made his call-backs, using the phone brought to him on an extension lead by the waiter.

Last call, when the action was set up, went to Councillor Mrs. Bagster. Jokey, debarred from fiddling with his knife in public, fiddled instead with his wineglass until the waiter had oiled up again on his flat and soundless veteran feet, and taken the phone away. Then he said, knowing the answer—obviously, Frankie had some hold over her; but he didn't share every secret—:

"How'd you know the old bint'll cooperate?"

"She'll cooperate, boyo," Frankie said. "Don't you worry about that. She'll cooperate."

Of course she would. Did he not hold in his possession a series of interesting photographs in glorious color, showing Councillor Mrs. Bagster, wife to the richest grocer in town, renowned for her social works and bookies' nap for next year's mayor, naked but for thigh-length leather boots, great breasts amuck as she plied a whip to two of Frankie's younger girls, picked up in a discreet bar and lying now bound and fettered and naked on a rug in a discreet flat? The man Herbert, who took the series through a hole cunningly devised in floor-length curtains, swore he never saw anything like it. And that from a man who'd seen a little. Her language was what impressed him. And Frankie, when the cassette was played back.

"It's bloody daft," said Jokey, "frigging about. The boy's got form, ain't he?"

"So's Maggie," Frankie told him, all easy smiles. "But only fines. From before she married Nobby. Soliciting. He made her give it up. Great loss to the profession."

"Well, then—for Chrissake—"

"Not in this town. They're not known in this town. The boy's still with the juvenile courts."

"He can check—"

"What, for a housekeeper? Why should he? Maggie will take care of him. She was an actress, remember?"

"Taking bloody stupid chances—"

"Drink up your wine," Frankie suggested, "and let's go home."

Accomplished operator though he was—and a man with his interests must be, to attract so little bird as he had served—Frankie could not be expected to know that before they left the table, trod over deep-piled carpet and were bowed out to where he turned the ignition key of a damson-colored Mercedes, the police knew every detail of his planning so far. But of the forthcoming job only. Nothing of his little prank. Only he and Jokey knew about that.

2

Detective Sergeant Alfred Stanley (Alf) Rosher was up to the elbows in suds next morning, when a knock came on the door. The bell was out of order, had been for a month, and he lacked the get-up-and-go to fix it. And now the washing machine seemed to have broken down. He had in it two pairs of underpants, three socks (he couldn't find the other one) and a couple of his shirts with the extra-long sleeve length, to cope with his gorilla-length arms; and quite suddenly it stopped thumping and went mute.

Well, it was not beyond his capacity, to fiddle about with an electric motor and even to get it working again; but he needed these things, supinely soaking now. Get 'em out, and rinsed, and on the line. Mend the sodding machine after. Or to hell with it. What did it matter, anyway? Let the bloody lot pack in, let the bloody house fall down, what did it matter? What did any bloody thing matter?

He opened the little round top. Too sudsy, in there. It usually was too sudsy, he never could shake out just enough of the powder. If he applied himself to more delicate shaking, it didn't go sudsy at all. Today, it was too sudsy. He rolled up his sleeves and inserted thick, hairy arms, groping; and just as he had everything gathered into a soaking wad dripping suds and water as he trotted with it to the sink, the knock came on the door.

The sink was filled with washing up. Another of the domestic phenomena he had discovered over the past three months: the sink is *always* filled with washing up. Even if you don't eat, it tiptoes back stealthily as soon as it is washed, wiped, stowed away, and the back is turned. So he dumped the sodden bundle down on the draining board, all among brown rings where cups of tea had stood and little pats of bacon fat gone adrift somehow from the frying pan, and wiped his hands on a dish towel wetter, if anything, than the bundle of clothes and the thick black hair on his arms. Then he answered the door.

On his doorstep, against the background of weeds where once was his trim little lawn and flowerbeds, stood two people he knew well enough. One was Councillor Mrs. Bagster, in a square tweed suit that bulged at the bust and a surprisingly frivolous hat decked with daisies; and the other the local vicar, the Reverend Pew (truly), five-feet-four in his thick black socks. Which he knitted himself, as a hobby.

"Ah," said Councillor Mrs. Bagster. Her well-dentured beam was strangely nervous. "Ah, good morning, Serg—er—Mr. Rosher."

"Good morning, Councillor," said Detective Sergeant Rosher. "Good morning, Vicar."

"Ah, yes," the vicar piped. "Good morning indeed. Yes. Yes, indeed."

And it was a beautiful morning, all the birds singing among the sun-happy trees, all the lovely flowers nodding benignly to drunk-on-nectar bees. Sergeant Rosher had not even noticed it. He did not notice it now. He murmured agreement, for politeness' sake, and waited.

"We—er—," said Councillor Mrs. Bagster, "we—er—thought we'd come to see you." Her beam was wide.

"Yes," the vicar concurred, "Yes. Indeed."

"About your advertisement."

16

"Ah."

A moment of silence. The vicar spoke, piping up of his own volition. "Perhaps we might—step in for a moment? —won't keep you—" "Yes. Yes," said Sergeant Rosher, drawing aside. The councillor, the vicar moved forward. The door closed, shutting out the humming, singing radiance. Rosher led on, into a living room cluttered with three months of masculine lone-living. "What can I do for you?" he asked.

"Your advertisement." Councillor Mrs. Bagster had a voice that went well with tweed. A sort of barking tone in it, especially when she was nervous. "I spotted it. Last night. Thought I'd have a word with the vicar. He agreed."

"Absolutely," said the vicar, nodding to confirm that this was an accurate presentation of the facts. When his hat was off, one found that the bush of gray hair thrusting out from under the brim stopped not far above the ears, giving way to a pink and pointed pate. The effect was quite peculiar.

No surprise touched Sergeant Rosher's mind at the obvious nervousness of these sudden callers. People who had not seen him since his calamity invariably showed awkwardness in his presence. They removed themselves from it as soon as they could. He was well steeled against them by now. And vicars, of course, are normally nervous.

"Are you suited?" asked the councillor.

"Pardon?" he said.

"Is there—the vacancy—is it filled?"

"Oh. No. I've had a couple of answers." One last night—a middle-aged woman who came to the house, quite obviously half drunk; and a telephone call this morning from a woman who surely could not have been drunk so early in the day, and so must have been more than half mad. Domestic help is not easily come by, in times when no woman starves if she won't take it up.

"Ah. Well, we have a problem—a woman, you know." Councillor Mrs. Bagster's surprisingly fine eyes beamed above her bared plastic gums. Behind their crinkling, the depths of them held nervous ingratiation. In the days of his honed sharpness, when almost every human action and reaction carried to him intimations of guilt, Rosher would have wondered why. But Rosher nowadays was too centered in his own despair, too self-absorbed, too focused on his own humiliation to notice what other people were up to. He didn't even care. Sod people. Sod police work. He plodded on toward retirement and a reduced pension with all his springs broken, simply because—well—what else can a man do, if he doesn't blow his brains out?

"Uh-huh," he said, and performed a ritual very well known down at the station. He produced with a flourish an enormous handkerchief, rumpled and gray where once all his linen had been scrupulously presented, and blew into it a klaxon blast that had the vicar shying nervously like a pink-pated pony. Mopped up, he put the handkerchief away; coughed and scratched the bald spot on the crown of his head. Really, the vicar thought, he *is* a coarse man. And so like a gorilla. Rosher stood unsmiling before them, blinking his hard little eyes. The vicar said:

"A sad case. A very sad case."

"Ah," said Rosher.

A pause. The councillor spoke again. "She was referred to me by a friend. Social Services, you know. I am, of course, chairman of the—er—of various committees." Oh, he's a hard-looking man, suspicious by nature. Look at his eyes. He'll check, he's bound to check. You're mad, to be here. But what can you do? Don't specify any particular service, don't name a definite committee. "A—er—battered wife. Brutal. Last night—badly beaten. Came home drunk. The husband, not her. Night before last, I mean, of course—I saw her yesterday. Nowhere to go—she had to leave the home—and of course, we have no hostel—"

"Why didn't she call the police?"

"Ah." Of course. Of course, he'd think of that, at once. He's a policeman. "Yes. I—she didn't think of it. I asked her that, naturally. She says all she thought about was getting away. From him. Her sister lived here. But when she got here, she'd moved. The sister, I mean. No forwarding address."

"Did she try the post office?

"Er—yes." Oh, God—it'll never stick. It's all getting so complicated. Oh, I wish I'd never seen a whip. "Apparently they—the sister and her family—went to Ireland."

"Ah."

"The fares and everything," the vicar put in. "She has no money. And subsistence—for herself and the two children—it all adds up. And, of course, if means were found to transport them, there is no certainty that the sister has room for them."

"Even," said the councillor, eased somewhat by his helping her out, "if she would take them in. Apparently they are not very close."

"Quite so," murmured the vicar. Really, there is no fool like an old fool, a sentimental clergyman with a comfortable living. The tougher men who carry the cross in slummy parishes are much less gullible.

"Children?" said Rosher.

The councillor's beam widened. "Quite large ones, not likely to be any trouble. A girl. Thirteen. And a boy. He's fifteen, I think she said."

"Fifteen, yes." The vicar nodded. "Charming children. Absolutely charming." Councillor Mrs. Bagster's beam embraced him. She felt for him a sudden wave of near affection. He'd been so much easier than this hard man. She didn't know how she would have managed, without him.

"Hrumph," went Rosher. His well-known grunt. Out came the gray handkerchief again and the vicar quivered before the blast. Away handkerchief; a coughing, and the extended finger at the end of an upraised arm, scratching at the hole in the hair. "I only want a woman. To keep things straight."

"Yes," said the councillor. "But we were thinking—the vicar and I, that is—that somebody living in your spare rooms—it's quite a large house, isn't it? And, of course, it would save you a good deal in salary. Housekeepers don't come cheaply nowadays. Do they? Two birds with one stone, perhaps."

Thought was moving in Rosher's stone-faced and strikingly

simian head. When he asked his policemanly questions it was purely by reflex action and not, as the councillor's nerves told her, from suspicion or even interest. But having inserted his advertisement at a time of peak domestic chaos and despair, he had since realized that his salary would never stretch beyond a woman shuffling about with the Hoover for a couple of hours a day. A living-in housekeeper competent to do what his fat wife used to do—he could feed her, but he couldn't pay her very much. The thought of all that money going out—even if he had it—twittered his mind already. What he needed, from every point of view, was exactly this: a woman living in, and working cheap.

And it was true: His was a large enough house, bigger than he intended it to be when he bought a semi-detached half of it and moved in with his young and pretty bride many years ago, to get her and himself away from police accommodation. Dirt cheap it was then, an old stone cottage gone to seed, set above what was virtually a village suburb still, beyond the town over which it looked. No other houses for a hundred yards down the hill, a quarter of a mile going up; and the other half occupied and owned by a little old lady with a gnashing chin, a rheumy eye, and gray grime in all the folds and crevices of her aged, aged skin. When she died, he was offered her half of the building cheap, by an heir who preferred booze to property. He bought it. Would have been a fool to have turned it down.

Since then, he had done a lot of work on it. He had intended to knock down the entire wall separating the two living rooms, thus making one enormous lounge; but it turned out that this wall was integral support, to remove it might well collapse the upper part of the house down into the lower. So he made a door through instead; which gave him now two identical lounges; one kitchen on this side; and a small room called the study, adapted (plus a little lavatory) out of the kitchen that used to be on the other side.

Upstairs were four bedrooms, each house having held two;

one of them made very small when he truncated it to build in the bathroom/bog. All this work he did with his own hairy hands; not from passionate do-it-yourself compulsion—no joy in marriage means no joy in the home—but because the man is a halfwit who does not realize, seeing the market trend, that improvement to his house is solid investment. Nothing better.

Now he stood in one of the two living rooms, both of which, like the rest of the rooms, showed very clearly how domestic standards head rapidly downhill without the deft hand of Woman on the brake, and said dubiously: "Hmm. Hummph. Is she clean? This woman?" He'd known bashed-up wives, in his time. Home life got out of hand is a recurrent theme in police work. In his opinion, half of them asked for it. Fag-smoking sluts with holes in their wrinkled stockings.

"Oh, yes. Yes," the councillor assured him eagerly. "Yes, indeed. Spotless. Very much the domesticated type."

"What about these—er—youngsters?"

"Charming," the vicar said. "A little—quiet, of course. A trifle withdrawn. Only to be expected, under the circumstances."

"Hmm. Hrrm." Rosher stood for a moment, frowning in thought. Then he added: "Well, no harm in having a look at 'em, I suppose."

The vicar beamed now, enthusiastically matching Councillor Mrs. Bagster's plastic effulgence. "I'm sure you won't regret it," he said. In his mind, quite obviously, mission was accomplished.

"I'm not promising anything."

"No, no—naturally," said the vicar. "But one does hope—if you feel you cannot—er—bring yourself to—I'm afraid it will mean splitting the family up. Such a dreadful pity, one always thinks. Terrible repercussions. Delinquency and so on." That should nail a policeman.

The fate of this or any other family did not unduly trouble Sergeant Rosher. Long observation had convinced him that most of them self-manufactured whatever fate befell. Forced into the sort of corner where the mote in one's own eye is clearly seen,

21

he even admitted that the rule applied to himself and all the family he had: his fat wife. But his domestic needs were pressing. So he said:

"Where are they now?"

"At the vicarage." The vicar seemed, suddenly, to have blossomed as chief apologist in the affair. "I can fetch them—in a few minutes—"

"Not now," said Rosher. "I'm just off to work. Soon after one o'clock." He would come home at lunchtime, instead of spending his hour chewing stolidly at something in thick brown gravy behind a propped-up newspaper in his usual café. He stayed away from the station canteen. Too much awkwardness, too many men trying to avoid his eye and his table, overjovial as they urged their mates to move up and make room where less embarrassment sat.

"Splendid," said the councillor, coming into her own again; and the vicar echoed: "Splendid!" The only one not beaming was Rosher. A long time, since anybody saw the baring of his brownstone teeth. In the very best of his good old days, he never was a man who beamed easy. He said:

"Now—if you'll excuse me—"

"Of course, of course," they said, and submitted to being shown out. Councillor Mrs. Bagster, walking away, found it difficult not to veer off course into the vicar, owing to shaky thick legs. And when she spoke briefly to Mad Frankie Daly a few minutes later, from a call box on her way home, the sweat from her clammy hands made wet patches on the telephone. "It's done," she said. That was all. But when she got back into her car, and all through the day, she was fighting against her own mind; telling it: He's not going to be robbed. It'll be all right—it's just a joke, that's all . . . . When they were gone, Detective Sergeant Rosher took up his soggy washing and dumped it into a bowl, unrinsed. If a woman was coming in, she could deal with that. He spread a crust with marmalade—it was all the bread in the house—and munched it standing amid the chaos of his kitchen. An indisputable truth about marmalade: It cannot be

22

confined entirely to the bread. So when he had munched, he rinsed his sticky hands under the tap and dried them on a dirty towel. The corner of the towel he used to remove the lump that fell on his shirt. Then he donned his jacket, settled low upon his stern brow his black Anthony Eden hat, and went to work.

At about the time when he arrived and settled his barrel-chested, thick body on the chair that did not fit his buttocks, stoically narrowing his mind to another day of small thefts and typewritten reports and all the little matters that settle on minor desks in CID rooms, from the office that used to be his—further along a corridor that clacked less since they put rubberized flooring down—came a man who felt the most acute embarrassment in his presense: Detective Inspector Cruse, promoted to fill the gap caused by Rosher's fall into his place. Cruse was Detective Sergeant, working under Rosher on the case that laid him low. He was first man on the scene when the incident happened, and so forced to give evidence at the enquiry.

Not by his own will did he find himself in Rosher's old office; but the Chief Constable was a hard man, with no consideration for trivialities like embarrassment and humiliation. Humiliation he probably welcomed, when it piled upon Rosher. The transfer applied for had not come through. By his implied instructions unorthodox efforts were made to keep Rosher out of court; but it was not done for love of him. It was because trial of a ranking policeman in a public court attracts unfavorable publicity, especially when sex is involved. So he kept the man from that, and bust him down. Given his way he would have castrated him. But there is no official procedure laid down for it, in the rule book. He settled for the next best thing, if indeed it was he who blocked the Sergeant's request for transfer.

To this hard man's office went Inspector Cruse, summoned by intercom. Up the stairs to the coconut matting and across it. Tap with the knuckles and wait. Open the door upon the command and move the feet onto carpet.

"Good morning, sir," said Inspector Cruse.

"Morning. Morning," the Chief Constable barked, and kept his massive, wire-haired head bent to his desk, scratching away with his golden pen. Paperwork—paperwork—paperwork. The ultimate bane of policemen, be they high or never so humble. A silence. When the craggy head lifted, the interview did not last long. No reason for it to do so, and this man did not waste words. He barked—not intending to, particularly, but because his was the kind of voice that barks willy-nilly; unlike that of Councillor Mrs. Bagster, which did it only when she was nervous:

"You wanted to see me, Inspector?"

"Yes, sir." The intercom summons came to Cruse in response to his request for an interview, to be passed from switchboard to Chief Constable as soon as he arrived. "Frank Daly. He's planning a big one." Even the names of criminals took on a certain regimental formality, spoken to the Chief Constable.

"Uh-huh. Information received?"

"Information received, sir." Which means a little man, whispering in a secluded rendezvous with a hand held out; or as in this case, a telephone call, often to a specified officer and no other. "He gathered his team last night, out at the Windmills."

"Uh-huh." The Chief did not ask who grassed. Every man's little men are his own affair, their identity a personal and close secret. "What's the job?"

"Not known yet, sir. Apparently he always gives a sort of preliminary dinner, just to get the boys together and put them on standby. So to speak." To no other man in this living world would Cruse have used a phrase like "so to speak." It just goes to show. He even used it after a full-stop pause, as if the speech felt unfurnished without it.

"Personnel?"

"I've got a list of names, sir. I'll let you have them."

"Good. Good. Your feller keeping you posted, is he?"

"Right along the line." Frankie did not know it, but he had among his band of brethren one who hated him as Cain hated Abel.

24

"Good. When's the action?"

"No definite date given. Just standby instructions. Maybe a week, maybe a bit more, my man says. He says Daly usually gives his dinner about a week ahead. We'll get all the details, as we go along." From the little man; or if he repented and failed to ring again: no matter. Given this initial lead, the police would be operating independently. Perhaps, without his muttering whisper from an untraceable call box, they would not know what was said at further meetings; but they'd know when and where they took place, and could look forward to being in at the finish with reasonable confidence.

"Uh-huh. All right, Inspector. Keep it under your hat for now; we'll call people in as we need them. Advise me as you go on."

Down went the Roman senator head again, the pen took up its burden of appending bold signature to memo and report and all the necessary bumph. Knowing his man, Inspector Cruse believed rightly that he was dismissed. No word of commendation or approval. The Chief rarely praised. A policeman's job is to catch criminals, isn't it, when he's not frigging about with parked cars? And what's so commendable about a phone call? "Sir," he said, and turned smartly from the big desk, checking the impulse to throw a salute. Pity, perhaps, that he was not even born, when men went soldiering for the last war. He could have been very good at it.

Now he would go back to the office that used to encompass the gorillaness, battleship gray raincoat and black Homburg hat of Detective Inspector Rosher, today huddled doggedly at a sergeant's desk in the unprivate CID room. From this office he would do the things Rosher had often done.

Some of the tradesmen calling at Mad Frankie Daly's apartment block from now would not be exactly what they appeared; unobtrusive men would walk about on pavements, here and around the homes of all the men named by the whisper on the telephone. Eyes would be watching, all round the clock. This arranged, Inspector Cruse would type the names list with his own two fingers and take it up on his own two feet to the Chief Constable, by now tying fishing flies against the day he would need them. It helped concentration. He said.

At one o'clock precisely, Detective Sergeant Rosher eased his cramped hams from the hard little chair—too bloody small, those chairs; everybody said so when they arrived, but what can you do?—and meticulously covered his typewriter. The fact that somebody would need to immediately uncover it again made no difference. In adherence to the laid-down rules he was meticulous, with the dogged defiance of the man who will not be faulted on *that*, whatever the buggers are saying. If this was his job he'd do his bloody job, and sod the lot of them. Typewriters will be covered when left unattended, it said. So he covered his typewriter and went, with no jovial comment from his colleagues such as usually accompanies the departure of a man off for lunch, or leave, or to pursue enquiry at a suspected brothel; to the row of pegs where hangs your common CID man's outdoor clothing. He shrugged into his battleship gray raincoat, settled his black hat, broke wind—a diet of boiled eggs and baked beans fulminates remarkably—and left the station.

Not really raincoat weather. A fine day, fifth in a row. For almost a week it had neither rained, snowed, nor blown a gale. On the Met Office roof they were breaking out the champagne, toasting the lovely sunshine.

Sergeant Rosher had no quickening of the blood from it as he moved on bowed legs incompetently fashioned, if they were meant to match his frame, to where his car stood. He inserted himself behind the wheel and drove away, through the town and up the hill to his house.

The vicar was there already when he came up the path between his sadly neglected flowerbeds, standing on the front step with the woman and two children, all looking slightly lost. "Ah, there you are, Mr. Rosher," he cried. "I was wondering if I had mixed—. I do sometimes, you know. Nothing for me to arrive at a Mothers' Union meeting on Wednesday instead of—yes. My poor wife used to say, I'd forget my head if—ha, ha. Well, here

26

we are." He rubbed his hands together, smiling a wide and nervous, almost pleading smile, as if it were he who needed desperately to make a good impression. No sign of Councillor Mrs. Bagster. She had used pressing council business as excuse to dodge the column.

"No mixup, Mr. Pew," said Rosher. "I said soon after one." And he bent his hard little eyes on the woman and her brood of two.

3

When Margaret Brian took that first call from Frankie in the small office of the discreet brothel in Birmingham, which brought him in surprising profit, and he asked if she remembered Rosher, the deep hatred she carried for that man burst in her veins like black fire. It was a rare day when she used unladylike language, except toward Rosher in her mind; but she said like a cat spitting:

"Remember him? The bastard. The bastard. Murdered Nobby, didn't he? One day I'll—I'll—"

"Yes, I know, me darling," said the lovely Irish brogue. "That's why I thought of you. How'd you like to help me set him up?"

"You? Set him up?"

"Yes."

"Finish him, do you mean?"

The voice wore its underlying chuckle. "Yes."

"How? Kill him?"

"No. I haven't worked all the details out yet; the thought just came to me, something I saw in the paper. You and me together, I think we can finish him off. Interested?"

"Oh, yes," she said; and in it was all the viciousness built up through the five years of her widowhood, out of loneliness and the pain of deep, deep grief. "My God, yes!"

"All right, me love. I'll ring you back. No need to hover over the phone—I have to give the matter a little thought. No hurry."

"I'll be here," she said.

"Right—good girl. I'll be back. How's business?"

Briefly, knowing this was merely a sort of courtesy question— knowing, most certainly, better than to start prattling about how much was coming from five staff girls and the odd free-lance arrangement at peak times—she told him: "Fine."

"Good," said Frankie. "Good. I'll ring you back, then. Look after yourself, my darling." Click went the phone, at the other end.

It was late evening when he rang again; and this is the busy time, in brothels. On all her available fornicating beds the buttocks were rising and falling, and in the lounge used as waiting room sat an elderly gentleman with a wobbly eye, who came once a week, in both senses of the word; this being all he could manage, and only with Collette (born Hilda Sims), who had the trick of persuading it; a nonconformist parson in mufti who, when it was over, left always a small wad of tracts beside the bed; and a man who was a well-thought-of customer when sober, but a bloody nuisance if he'd had a few, as he'd had tonight. The big, broken-nosed man lounging in the easy chair was Jim, stationed there to keep an eye on him. A valued staff member, Jim. Once a heavyweight title hope until an ex-gratia payment and ten seconds on his back cost him his license. Capable all alone of subduing the odd rambunctious drunk or recalcitrant and keeping him that way until he could be bundled into a plain van and dumped, in the small hours, nicely terrorized, ten miles out among the cows.

She was in the bright kitchen, supervising the brewing of tea (or coffee, choice lay with the client. The nonconformist parson always took tea), ready access to which is a feature of well-run cathouses, where it is acknowledged that fornication is thirsty work; when the black girl Myra, off-duty tonight because of the time of month and so stationed in the office to give her something to do, came to her and said: "Wanted on the phone, Mrs. Bental. Welsh or something, he sounded like."

"Thank you, Myra," said Margaret, and followed the neat, swaying buttocks which, bared for business, looked like a coffee-flavored meringue, out and along the nicely decorated, scrupulously cleaned and polished hall to the trim little office. Here she said into the phone, having waved hovering Myra out of the room: "Hallo?"

"Maggie," said the well-fed voice from the dinner table. "Hallo again, my love. I've set a little thing up. Shall I tell you all about it now?"

"Yes," she said.

"Well, I spotted this advertisement, do you see. Our friend wants a housekeeper. How do you fancy being a housekeeper?"

"I don't follow," she said.

"No. Well, you wouldn't, would you? All right, let me elucidate. You know they bust him down, don't you?"

"Yes." And black rejoicing she'd felt at it. She and many others.

"And you know his wife left him?" Professional and domestic calamity in a copper's life is pure, pure joy to the bent. They follow developments avidly, chortling over their jugs. Or hand-tooled glasses if status decrees that they drink short out of such, or they recently lifted a load of mixed crockery. And there is a grapevine, to paint in the picture for those once harassed here now living—perhaps as result of that harrying, applied by the copper involved—in other towns.

"Yes."

"Well, he's been living on his own ever since. Now he wants a woman."

"In bed?"

"Well now, I expect so. He always was a lecherous old basket. Wasn't he?"

"Was he?"

"Didn't he run his ruler over you?"

"I only saw him a couple of times. At a distance."

She didn't even attend Nobby's trial. Strangely, because Nobby was a man with small capacity for tenderness, the love she bore him he reciprocated. He kept her cozy, away from his business; and when it came to his trial he said he didn't want her there, it would unsettle him. Perhaps this was partly because things would be bandied that he didn't want her to know about. So she stayed away.

"Would he know you, do you think?"

"I don't know. I doubt it, I never met him. And Nobby was very particular about no photos. In clubs and places."

The two glimpses of Rosher had been caught on occasions when, in secret defiance of orders, she sneaked away in the morning to hang about outside the court to see her beloved Nobby when they bustled him in from the prison van. She kept well away on the far side of the street; and she wore a dark wig over the bright blonde hair that Nobby loved, and a nondescript hat over that. An equally nondescript coat, and if Nobby had glanced her way he would never have known her. Simple enough, for a girl who once earned her living as an actress. Wigs don't cost much nowadays, and she bought the clothes for under a pound, in a secondhand shop. Not that she lacked money, with Nobby; but she was a natural housewife. She didn't throw his money about, it was all he could do to coax her into paying once a week to keep her hair bright yellow. And he honored her for it.

"You had your blonde hair then, didn't you?"

"Yes." She knew what he meant. Long yellow hair is a thing likely to stick in a randy man's mind. If Rosher ever saw her, and knew her for Nobby's wife, blonde hair would be the thing that rose into his memory even though, as a seasoned copper, he knew about wigs and color rinses and letting it all grow out; which is what she had done, reverting to her natural mid-brown after Nobby's death. She never had liked it yellow, she wore it for him. She said now: "He wouldn't know me."

"That's what I was thinking, darling. Especially if you dab on a little bit of this and a little bit of that. You'd better have a black eye, for a start. And a couple of abrasions. Think you can manage that?"

"What's it all about?" she demanded. The man was going around in Irish circles. A race of talkers, the Irish. Seldom come straight to the point except when they suddenly knock you flat, in a pub.

"I've fixed for you to get the job, darling. Battered wife. You'll have two children. Right?"

"What children?"

"You'll meet 'em. At the Harley Road bus station—they'll be waiting for you. You'll go to The Pines, in Dinsmore Avenue—big house, stands in its own grounds. Councillor Mrs. Bagster. She'll take you to the vicar of St. Marks. I don't know what she's got worked out exactly, but she'll see to the details. You'll need a name. Let's see, now . . . Mrs. Loving." The voice took on that irresistible chuckle. "Yes—I like that. Mrs. Loving. O.K.?"

"Yes, but—what am I supposed to do?"

"Nothing, darling. Just get in there. Play it demure. Once you're in—you think about it. We can fill his house up with baubles. Then we tip off his bosses."

"So what happens to me? I mean—I'm in there, with all these baubles—"

"You'll be gone, darling. Won't you?"

"It won't stick," she said. "They'll know it's a plant—"

The chuckle again. "Probably. But they'll have to hold an enquiry, won't they? And we see to it that the newspapers know. If it sticks, he's done for. If it doesn't: Well, what the hell's a copper doing, letting it all happen? Not going to do him any good, is it, another enquiry? He'll be done for that way, too."

No need to tell her one child was a crook well known in his hometown of Bradford, the other chief delight of the shabby-raincoat brigade in a series of pornographic films and photographs. No need to remind her that she herself, way back when she was a struggling rep actress with sudden desperate need to augment her pittance, acquired by reason of amateur incompe-

32

tence two convictions in Hull for soliciting. Two juvenile delinquents and a whore in the house: This alone would take a lot of explaining, when Rosher stood again under the Chief Constable's unmerciful eye. Whatever happened, there would be fun in it for the fraternity, and a nod of admiring approval for the joker who set him up.

"It won't stick—" she said again; but he broke smoothly in:

"You let me worry about that, darling. O.K.?"

When Frankie commanded she felt obliged to obey, quite apart from the fact that he did not like to have his orders—sweet spoken though they may be—turned down. He had been very good to her in the time of grief, giving her this job and all. And any chance to hit the hated Rosher was a thing to grasp firmly.

"Wait while I take down the address," she said; and did so, on the pad used for noting appointments. Many clients preferred a discreet call, naming a certain girl to a probable wait in the lounge, followed by a coupling with whoever first became available, or an even longer wait for the preferred servicing. "When do you want me to go?"

"Now, more or less," he said, "if there's a coach. Arrive in the small hours—it always looks good. Cheap suitcase, if you can find one—you know how to present it."

"What about the business?" she asked. "We're pretty busy."

"Hand it over to Gladys, darling. She can hold the fort." Gladys, called Estrellita. Head girl, and specialist in the twenty-fifth position.

So now she stood with the vicar, flanked on Rosher's doorstep by the two youngsters met for the first time when the late-night coach from Birmingham drew up after midnight at the Harley Road bus station, and the heart beat up in her, mixing nervous tension with a choking surge of hatred as the sergeant left his car and came apelike, but with all the old elasticity gone from his walk, through the gate and up the weedy path. She thought:

That's him, the bastard. He looks older—they've kicked the bounce out of him. And sick. He looks sick. I hope he dies of it, the murdering bastard. The bastard.

The vicar, beaming his ingratiating goodwill to all men, cried:

"Ah, there you are, Mr. Rosher. I was wondering if I had mixed—. I do sometimes, you know. Nothing for me to arrive for a Mothers' Union meeting on Wednesday instead of—yes. My poor wife used to say, I'd forget my head if—ha, ha. Well, here we are." He rubbed his hands together and looked like a praying mantis.

"No mixup, Mr. Pew," said Rosher. "I said soon after one." And he bent his hard little eyes upon her brood of two.

She looked decent enough. Not pretty, exactly, but then he wasn't choosing a beauty queen. Comely, she might have been called, even in her brown and respectable coat, a demure hat worn on mid-brown hair, an old cheap suitcase standing by. One black eye she had. Marks of recent abrasion on a cheek, and a small piece of sticking plaster adorned her chin. The youngsters, too, seemed docile enough: a very pretty young girl at the stage of uprising breasts and widening hips, a rather long-haired but good-looking lad a year or two older. Both wore the ubiquitous jeans and tee shirts, the girl topped off with a colored anorak. The boy wore a mock-leather jacket, short and elasticated at the waist and with a sheepskin collar that never saw sheep or shepherd.

"This is Mrs. Loving," the vicar said.

"Ah," said Detective Sergeant Rosher, without lightening of the stern brow. "How d' yuh do."

"And this is Helen. And Tommy."

"Hi," the girl child said, pretty white teeth showing in a smile. Only a grunt came from Jimmy Burt.

"Uh-huh." The sergeant nodded briefly. After a moment, he added: "Well, we'd better go in."

He opened one of his two front doors—the other, of course, was at the far end of the building, separated from here by the front windows of his two living rooms—and stood aside. The vicar leaped to commandeer the suitcase as the woman bent to lift it and they all filed past, into the house. He closed the door as they stood with the overdressed, indecisive look of strangers in his undusted passage, and opened the interior one to usher them into the cluttered lounge. It smelt frowsy, he realized suddenly. "Better sit down," he said.

They sat, the two youngsters side by side on his settee, the woman primly upright on the edge of one of the big easy chairs. The vicar remained standing, beaming among his surprising side-hair under a gleaming pate. "I understand," the policeman said stiffly, "that you wish to apply for the post of housekeeper."

"Yes," she said.

"Ah. Mm." Rosher was not sure how to proceed, having never been in the situation before. What questions did one ask before one said when can you start clearing this lot up and cooking a decent meal? "I see. Mm. You—er—Councillor Mrs. Bagster informs me you are having—er—domestic problems."

"Yes." Very quietly. But composed.

"The post is—er—permanent. Subject to satisfaction. On both sides. Naturally." No starting today and sudden tearful reconciliation with hubby leaving me back in the proverbial shit by Saturday, is what he was really saying.

She understood him. "I need a permanent post," she said, adopting his stilted, archaic phrase demurely, almost submissively. Soft, her voice. Submissive was, perhaps, the word for her, sitting upright with her hands folded in her lap, unaggressive in personality as an Oriental woman. A good actress, and one well versed in the psychology of the male. You cannot madam a brothel for nigh on five years without learning a thing here, a thing there. It all adds up. Bulky and domineering men like submissive woman. She sat folded together, hands together, knees together, quietly awaiting his lordly pleasure.

"Not much likelihood of—I think," the vicar said.

"Hmm," said Rosher. "Hrumph." He produced his great gray handkerchief and set all the motes panicking on the dusty air with one phenomenal blast. The boy's eyebrows went up at the shock of it, the girl smothered a sudden giggle, turning into cough before it had time to identify itself. The vicar blinked, but was not completely shattered, having passed this way before. Only the woman absorbed without tremor.

The Sergeant wiped, tucked away the sheet, coughed, and scratched with his thick forefinger where hair had departed from his durable skull. "Mm," he said. "Hrrrmph. I wasn't thinking of—er—." He glanced at the children; sat for a moment, ruminating. At last he said: "Mm. About salary—I'm not in a position to—er—"

"A home is what I really need," she said quietly. "Where we can all be together."

Mentally, the vicar breathed a sigh of relief. When the salary comes under discussion, bar sudden calamity, only the details remain to be settled. He could report to Councillor Mrs. Bagster that all was safely gathered in. Delicately sensitive to every social nicety, as befits a man of the cloth, he eliminated himself before the subject broached must be expanded before his ears. "If you will forgive me—really must run—jumble sale this afternoon. Mustn't leave the ladies to cope with everything, eh? Some of the jumble is quite heavy. Yes. I'll leave you to your discussion. Splendid." And off he went, almost bobbing on the doorstep as he thanked Rosher with moisture in his honest eyes.

It did not take long, to fix the details. She would draw a small salary, not much more than pocket money. Two weeks' trial. They would choose between bedrooms, she and the girl, and the boy would have the little one; leaving Rosher with his own room. In return, she would take over the shopping, cooking, cleaning, and all household duties. The second living room would be theirs. Food, he would provide.

He showed them the rooms—they were in fair order, if a little dusty, because he never went near them—and she pronounced herself well satisfied, and very grateful. And all this time the youngsters said not a word. When they were back again in his living room, he spoke with the stiff awkwardness that had taken over, of late, from his old-time bombast.

"Well, I'd better be getting back to work. Perhaps you'd like to—um—start in straightaway. There's tea and so on in the kitchen cabinet. I'll be back about six."

"Yes," she said, in her soft voice. "Yes—all right. Thank you."

He drove back to the station, and as he attended automatically to the task of easing the car through the town center traffic, he thought: Hadn't intended to take kids. But the old girl who came the other night won't do, and nor will the one who rang yesterday. Nobody else has applied. And she seems clean enough. And I can afford her. Well, give it a trial. If it lasts only two weeks the place will be cleaned up a bit. And I might have some decent grub inside me. Gave her a fair pasting, the husband, by the look of it.

In his living room when he was gone, the girl called Helen (it was her real name; she had no record, there was no reason to change it) threw herself, sprawling, into his favored armchair. "Phew," she said, grinning. "Poor old sod. Anybody got a fag?"

Margaret was well used to handling the type. "There'll be no fags for you, my girl," she said, very crisply. "You play it the way Frankie wants it, or I ring him. Understand?"

Still grinning, not really concerned with smoking but trying out adult reaction by pushing in a needle, as youngsters will, the girl said: "He's bloody miles away by now, Mother."

"It lingers. None of us smokes, you least of all."

"Sod that."

"And watch the language. I don't know what Frankie told you, but I know what he told me. Smoking and swearing don't fit it."

"Oh, Christ," the child said. "Hark at Mum."

The lad had been wandering, inspecting things. He was picking up one of Rosher's boxing trophies from the sideboard now, reading the inscription engraved on it. "Police Heavyweight Champion. Three years," he said, his vocal production mangled in the Bradford fashion. "The old guy's a bloody menace, ain't he? We're going to need brass knuckles, when he gets going." He weighed a cup in each hand. "Silver. Could be worth a bob or two, this lot."

"Lay off," said Margaret. Not difficult, when they dropped the assumed face, to assess these two. The boy, a small-time villain likely to progress to bigger things; the girl, conforming to the pattern sent by God to tempt schoolmasters. Had she known in ad-

37

vance how blatant they were, she might have thought twice about the caper. But then—Frankie was out to do Rosher, and she was blessed with a main part in it. "Right," she said, "let's get to work. We'll start on this room—give it a good going over. Then we'll do the kitchen."

The girl looked at her, open mouthed. "What?" A tone of utter disbelief. "*Work*? For *him*—for a bloody pig?"

And the boy said: "Not likely, mate."

Rosher spent the afternoon of that day as now he spent all his days. Out in the town and in other parts of the building men worked on more vivid matters; but he trudged on through paperwork related to the pettiest of all the crime that ebbs and flows through every police station, methodically, stoically whittling the pile from his IN tray, to reconstruct it in his OUT tray. In the office that used to be his, Detective Inspector Cruse, also stuck with paper as all CID men are from time to time, performed a similar trick; but at least he had the interior, comforting knowledge that something better was brewing, and some small break in the monotony when the newly appointed watchers over Frankie and his little band of helpers reported in after handing over to the relieving shift, saying no untoward movement had taken place. For Rosher, there was nothing but paperwork.

At five thirty—this was one of the weeks when he had a through-the-day shift—he eased his buttocks once more from his detested chair, again covered his typewriter, donned his black hat and battleship gray raincoat, and set himself for home.

When he got there and opened the front door he stopped dead on the threshold, fetched up short by cleanly order and cooking. The floor had surely been scrubbed and polished over? And the two rugs, lately gone a lank-haired and despondent gray—how had they become young again, white and fluffy? Oh, and quivering in the nostrils, bathing in immediate saliva the tough brown teeth that decorated his tough gums, a glorious savor of things cooking tenderly in scoured pots and ungreasy oven.

The belly of Sergeant Rosher gave rumbling tongue as he bore it across the hall and opened the door to his living room. Everything here, too, was restored to urbanity, a small fire laid in the grate, ready for lighting should chill come suddenly, as it does too often after a day of British summer. His slippers stood on the fire surround, rubbed free of collected dust, shampooed, perhaps, to remove accumulated grease from droppings when he fried bacon and hooked it out with a fork, to slap it between bread.

He moved across the carpet to the fireplace; automatically stretched out his hands as if to warm them. Not because they were cold, but because this transformation back to the domestic order prevailing in the days of his fat wife, this sudden focus on a new and strange woman's work in his house, took him out of stride. He needed a hand-warming second or two to reorient, before his mind accepted the fact that he had every right to remove his big, box-toed shoes, don his slippers, and sit in his own chair. He proceeded accordingly, and was halfway through the change when she knocked on the door with quiet knuckles, waiting until he invited before she came in, to stand just inside, saying:

"I was not sure what you wanted for dinner, Mr. Rosher, so I've made a steak and kidney pie, with a fruit salad to follow. Will that be all right?"

The stomach inside him clenched and unclenched like an agonized fist, it brayed another desperate rumble. "Ah," he said. "Yes. Yes. Very nice." Fruit salad was not exactly his thing, a good solid roly-poly pudding was what he loved best, washed down with plenty of dark mahogany tea; but steak and kidney pie . . .

"Good," she said. Very fresh-looking now, in a neat print frock with her black eye and abrasions newly touched up. "Perhaps you will tell me every morning what you'd like for dinner, and I'll get it during the day."

"Ah. Yes," he said, one shoe off, one shoe on. He donned a slipper; untied the lace of the remaining shoe. "You've—er—." It came hard, for Rosher to pay a compliment. "You've—I must say, you've made a good start. In here."

"Thank you." She was basing the character on books read,

films seen. A trifle passé, perhaps, the unobtrusive key; but a good performance overall. And given the relationship as established in earlier scenes, perhaps not too low pitched. Stomach almost as tautly mobile with hate as his with hunger, she added: "Would you prefer to eat in here, or in the kitchen?"

"Ah. The kitchen, I think." It had never occurred to him in all his years of residence to eat anywhere else. But you could, I suppose, he thought. Table up to the fire in here—somebody else to set it out, take it away after and deal with the washing up—very comfortable.

"It will be ready when you are."

She went quietly away, to dragoon her daughter in on the necessary presentation. A touching, cozy domesticity about a pretty little girl helping black-eyed and bashed-up Mummy, in haven at last after storm and stress. Where the boy was, she didn't know. He just buggered off, saying he was going out.

A few minutes later Rosher was seated in the miraculously gleaming and ordered kitchen, eating off so-clean china the glorious-scented, lightly golden-crusted pie flanked by three perfectly cooked vegetables, all served to him by a quiet and comely woman and a pretty little blonde in a school-type skirt, with breasts like small ripening pears under a white blouse. Part of her stock in trade, these clothes, worn with strapped shoes and short white socks. Popular character and always profitable to the presenters, the schoolgirl slowly stripped and moving on from virgin protest through near rape to enthusiastic and increasingly acrobatic participation.

But breasts, fledgling pear or come to mother-ripeness, held no attraction for Rosher now. Breast man he had always been, and a drooler over hip and buttock. All that was over. Tonight saliva flowed in tribute to the eunuch's chief compensation: food.

You could say that he was seduced by a steak and kidney pie. This, and cleanliness, and a long-missed domestic ambience; all at low cost. Basically, and especially now when she had reason to be, Margaret was a gifted cooking house tender. She looked well to the comfort of the late Nobby Brian, who, like many crooks (they learn appreciation in prison), placed high value on such domestic virtue. He loved her for this aspect of her talent as much as for her ability in bed; and God knows, he loved that, all right. As he had every right to do. Married her, didn't he?

But he should have checked. Rosher should. There are ways by which policemen can find out background details of people, even if they come from another town. He can at least learn whether they have form; and if they do, a great deal more than that, from files and telephone talk with officers who know them.

This is for sure: If they and their sponsoring councillor had been faced with the aggressive eye and acute suspicion of the old Rosher, they'd never have got inside the house; or if they did, it would have been by his gathering them together in a convenient place, for the chopper when his probing was complete. He would have smelled unsavory fish, as sure as eggs are ovoid.

But the old Rosher was gone. An aging shell lived here, plodding on to broken retirement, all his life a wreck around him. Behind the stone face dwelt the sort of crippled self-esteem that makes a man defer to people like Councillor Mrs. Bagster, hot tip for mayor, who seem to have made so much less cockup of their lives; and a deep revulsion against the work he had made the mainspring of his existence. That he remained a copper at all, in the wake of his humiliation, was due to two things only: Bust or not, he had still the fighter's blind instinct, his old dogged reaction to knockdowns. He wouldn't let the bastards finish him off. And then: the pension. Reduced, with his reduction in rank; but due in a couple of years, and all he would have to supplement his savings.

So he plodded on through his days of paperwork—constant freshening of humiliation, by decree of the unforgiving Chief Constable—and his soul rejected it all: the work that had been his shield against his fat wife and his power against his own aloneness, and the men he worked with arrogantly once, who met him now stony-eyed, or made uneasy jokes.

He checked nothing. Did not even ask for references. Offered

41

something warm and comforting, like a baby fresh nappy-changed, he reached blindly and with relief, to fasten onto the nipple. Which is why the boy Jimmy Burt was able, during his wandering about on a sizing-up tour of the town, to ring Frankie from a call box and say:

"We're in."

"Did I tell you to ring me here?" Frankie said. Amiably enough: To legally bug a man's phone is not as easy as crime writers would have you believe. It is a complicated matter, and there has to be strong reason for it. No such reason existed, in Frankie's opinion; but this personal number was not given to everybody, nor was it in the book. Familiar with the ways of the bent, he did not need to ask where the lad got it. Margaret had it, probably noted down. The little sod had been through her handbag. Well, boys will be boys.

"Thought you'd want to know," said Jimmy Burt. "Dead easy. Copper? He's a right old prick, ain't he?"

"Don't get cocky, sonny," snapped Frankie. "He was putting 'em away before you were born." He had no love for Rosher, but cocky young males are singularly irritating, to older males. Cocky older males, especially.

"Right old prick, he is," said Jimmy Burt. "Couldn't catch pussy." And he rang off, laughing.

Here is another thing Frankie didn't know: A whispered call after his dinner party had already set a magistrate's signature to permission for a tap on his telephone. Had he known, and automatically realized that the police must somehow have sniffed the wind, he would certainly have called the big job off, and so altered the whole course of Rosher's history and his own.

When Detective Inspector Cruse received the tape record and transcript, he mounted the stairs again to the Chief Constable's office. The Chief read the brief report, listened to the brief voice on the cassette, and said:

"Lancashire."

"Mm." Balls. That's Yorkshire. Lay you money on it.

42

"Copper? What copper?"

"I don't know, sir." It didn't say, did it?

"Mm," said the Chief Constable. "Interesting. From a call box."

"Yes." Public booth calls are traceable; but where is the caller, by the time you get there? "Mandeville Road post office."

"Yes, yes, yes." The Chief could read, it was all there on the small official form; which he handed back now to the Inspector. "Well, not much help, at present. You'll keep me posted." His mind was saying:

Copper? Bent? One of mine? Nothing to go on—could be any one of thousands, here or anywhere in the country. And in where?

Something to do with the coming job? Nothing to do with the coming job? An unrelated call?

Most likely. Phone tap—waste of time. Daly was too cagey to discuss his plan over the phone.

"Of course, sir." Cruse shared his chief's view of the phone tap. Nothing big would come out of it, not from a shrewd operator like Mad Frankie; but it had to be there, just in case.

"All right, Inspector," the Chief said. "That will be all."

Down the stairs yet again went Inspector Cruse, to his office; where he placed the report in the brand-new, as yet sparsely populated file neatly labeled and set aside to receive whatever bumph accumulated under the heading: DALY, FRANCIS PATRICK. Nothing to be done about it except so file it and include it in the thinking.

Couldn't investigate every copper for miles around. Perhaps the caller would ring again, and be more specific. Actually, it didn't read quite as though a copper were bent. More as if the caller was reporting, with normal criminal glee, wool pulled over his eyes.

4

It will never be eradicated while one of them is left alive, nor can it be gainsaid, the compulsion in the Irish to overdo things. Count John McCormack singing "Mother Machree," very scratchy by now but still played on BBC radio request programs aimed at the near senile, is a case in point. So is enthusiasm for holy murder in the matter of Catholic south and Protestant north, and the blarney of oldest inhabitants lovably cadging pints of Guinness from innocent American tourists and well-bellied West Germans who just bought the lake, around Killarney way.

It follows, then, as a Connemara sunset follows a Dublin Bay dawn—and both are infinitely overdone—that much of what Frankie did to set up Sergeant Rosher was extravagant and unnecessary.

Let it be acknowledged: A man with a hobby is entitled to let himself go on it. He can, in his enthusiasm, ignore professional rules such as he applies to his business, provided the hobby is undertaken for fun only. As with amateur actors. Many a bank manager, accountant, solicitor, his working day spent grave faced and beady eyed, struts and roars and rants like a maniac publicly in his spare time, and gains great pleasure by it.

So it was with Frankie. He felt no great animosity to Rosher, or to any other policeman. Some of his best friends had been Dublin policemen, until they were put away. The pigs in general were simply the enemy, that's all, and active soldiers do not usually hate the enemy.

But this was the first time ever that Frankie had found one so comically vulnerable; and when he explored the matter, he received a flash of light that told him there was more fun-potential here than he at first had realized. It no longer mattered—never had, very much—whether they bust Rosher again or not. Thing was: Laughter among the bent would last forever, the fixing of the once feared and hated Rosher by Frankie Daly, broth of a boy if ever there was one, would pass into legend—and on both sides of the law. Because Frankie, vanished to a sunny island a thousand miles away after this, the final big tickle, would see to it that the whisper filtered to the Chief Constable and all the policemen down to Charlie; much too late to do any of them any good. Up would go the lot of them, to dangle beside the hapless Rosher amid hoots of happy laughter from the side-split bent.

It need hardly be said that most of Frankie's phone calls, in or out, if they related to business were brief and noncommittal. When he needed to elaborate or a point demanded clarification, he called back from a public booth. This was not because he thought his phone might be tapped—a good criminal knows something of law—but because (a) one day it might be; and (b) you can never be absolutely certain no wires are crossed, causing some startled housewife to be receiving you when she picked up the phone to ring Edna. And operators bored at night have been known to listen in. Telephone discipline imposed rigorously upon self and associates could save a lot of trouble.

So Margaret, calling from Rosher's house the morning after arrival, when she had sent that man off to work clean-shirted and belly-furnished with grapefruit, eggs, and bacon (and a pork sausage), toast and marmalade, and about a gallon of hot, bitter-black tea, kept it brief. "Everything's going very well," she said.

45

"Good," said Frankie. "Very good. No problems?"

"No problems. I'm not too keen on my assistants, that's all."

He chuckled. "You'll get to love 'em. What shift is Dad on this week?"

"All day. About nine to five thirty. Home about six."

"Just so I know when to ring. Look after yourself, darling." That was it. Down phone. And this conversation, too, was reported to Inspector Cruse. It meant nothing much. Just one among several such calls made by or to Frankie during the day. Cruse put it into the file and waited. "Dad" was an obvious cover-word. Or was it? People have dads. No reason why Cruse, noting this call from a woman, should connect Dad with a copper mentioned by a Yorkshire male.

The next day Frankie rang Margaret; but this call was not recorded because he made it from a booth. He said:

"Darling—Frankie. The old man out?"

"At work." She wore her demure print dress. Over it a pinafore, one the fat wife had left abandoned in a cupboard; and upon her neat and attractive head—a thing about Margaret often remarked upon, her natural neatness—a head-scarf tied like a turban. In the time of his wonderful lechery, Rosher would have left for the office panting like a dog and wearing tight trousers.

"Good. Listen—I've been thinking. Has he made a play for you yet?"

"Him? He's past it. Food's what he wants—he nearly eats the pattern off the plates."

"Does he so? Well, he always was a dirty old man, wasn't he?"

"Was he? I never got near enough to find out."

"He was, darling, he was. Take my word for it. Noted, he was. It was a woman got him busted, wasn't it? And the leopard doesn't change his spots."

"This one has."

"No, no. He's been starving for food, I expect. And you cook like the Mother of God herself, darling. What's he been feeding on, all on his own?"

46

"I don't know, do I? I wasn't here. There's a lot of baked beans in the larder. And tinned sausage."

"Baked beans don't do much for a man, do they now? Feed him up a couple of days—he'll be back. He wouldn't be past it— not at his age. You know that."

She knew it. Back at the brothel, many a wizened old lecher bared his withered bum, groaning through rheumatic twinges as he risked heart seizure, prostrate collapse, and the chill that kills (although one did it in a shawl) in the quest for just one more climax, lest the Grim Reaper should cut it off forever in the night. But she made no comment. Instead, she asked:

"Why do you want to know?"

"I had the thought," said Mad Frankie, "that love is blind."

"So?"

"Well, now. If he fell for you he wouldn't be watching out for things, would he?" And a moonstruck Rosher would be the hoot among hoots. In folk history, he would be pictured simpering under slicked-down hair, blushing with a bunch of daisies. And all for a brothel madam.

"What things?"

"That, I haven't decided yet. But you see what I mean?" Oh, the perfect beauty of it. There the poor old feller would be, hoist again with his own penis. His house stuffed with loot, and he charged with offenses against a child.

"There's not a chance, Frankie," she said. "Not a chance. Besides, what do you want me to do? Sleep with him?" Flesh crawled at the thought. She'd do it, if it could be clearly demonstrated that the act would contribute heavily to Rosher's downfall; but the womb would cringe, and she didn't see what would be gained by it.

He knew her refusal, by the hardening of her tone. Pity—if she'd cooperated he might have insinuated Herbert into there, or stationed him up a tree with a telephoto lens, she to ensure that the curtains were left open. Collector's items, they'd be; snaps of Rosher grinding away stripped to the socks, color by Kodachrome. The Chief Constable would love 'em. Perhaps she'd come to it yet. But softly, softly. "No, no, darling," he said. "Nothing like that, if you don't fancy it. I just thought he might be—diverted, is all."

"Not a chance. He's off it altogether."

No man is ever off it altogether. He'd soon come on again, if you handled him right. And you know it. "All right, darling—forget about it. Just an idea. You carry on. Just carry on. I'll be in touch. On all day the whole of the week, is he? Good. Watch how you go, then."

The trouble with him, and all the type, she told herself as she put the phone down—once they get you into the setting, you never really know what they're up to.

She was not worried about it yet—to date, she hadn't considered it—but the truth is, hatred for Rosher had carried her away. When you deal with an Irishman who has earned for himself the tag Mad Frankie, you should find out before you commit yourself exactly what his plan is. If it's not all cut and dried—let it go. But there you are: Hatred can be as blinding as love. And Mad Frankie's whimsical humor did not color his business dealings. She never came up against amateur Frankie before.

The Irishman's next idea was pure whimsy, born in a billiard hall where he was passing a peaceable morning hour with Jokey Fenton after this talk with Margaret. Because he chuckled as he shot the black into a corner pocket, Jokey asked him what was funny. So he outlined. Jokey said:

"You're playing with bleeding fire. That's what you're doing—playing with bleeding fire."

"It's a poor heart," Frankie told him, "that never rejoices."

"You're going to rejoice too bloody often, the way you're carrying on," his narrow-headed little henchman said. It was making him uneasy, this caper. Stupid. It was bloody stupid.

"What happened to the spirit of adventure, boyo?"

"Listen," said Jokey, "you're not the only one involved in the tickle, you know. This fucking about—it's nothing to do with the job, is it? You owe something to the rest of us—"

"I owe nothing to you." A small snap, biting through the blarney-silk. "*You owe to me.* Never let you down yet, have I? Without me you wouldn't be wearing fancy underwear, and you'd have nobody but screws to see 'em. Have you got a twopenny piece about you?"

He rang Margaret again. Asked to speak to Jimmy Burt. When the lad came on the line—only just out of bed, lazy little tyke; Rosher would have looked down his broad and hairy-nostriled nose, had he known—the leader gave him the billiard hall public phone number and told him to call it back. The reason why he did this: Only one twopenny piece between him and the conversation-truncating pips; and whoever's phone might be tapped, it was unlikely to be Rosher's. So there was another call the police missed.

Two nights later—in the small hours of the day after, to be exact; it took that long to set it up—young Jimmy Burt stood tucked into an alley opposite Councillor Mrs. Bagster's shop, one of five all called Betty's Boutique, in company with a strangely wizened, humpty-backed little man named Bertie Smithers, small fry indeed among Frankie's circle of professional associates. They watched, well hidden, while the patrol car slid by, up the street and away. An hour they had, before it passed this spot again. Without a word, because words were superfluous, this was the moment they had been waiting for, Jimmy slipped across into the shadow of the boutique doorway.

There never was an easier break-and-enter than this, all set up from the inside. Councillor Mrs. Bagster's manager was not bent, exactly; but he did rely on dope, and Frankie controlled the supply. Councillor Mrs. Bagster had no idea the lad was a hooky; he did his work well enough, being also as queer as a cuckoo and in love with chunky near-jewelery and fashion clothing; any more than he realized a connection between his big, butch lady boss and the solacing of his own twittering need.

For that matter, had anybody mentioned Frankie Daly he would not have recognized the name. Even the sleazy addict-pusher from whom he bought his supplies—at increasing cost—

did not know who headed the local distribution chain, many links above him. Tiniest of mites in the international trade, Frankie was. Just another localized outlet. But it gave him certain power, and he had on file in his mind the names and addresses of all the little sniffers and smokers, with their trades. You never know who will be useful, and people suddenly deprived become desperate.

So it took no more than a couple of minutes to do the lock on the front door, and this was genuine. Jimmy had a talent for locks, and the men who started him off when he was small enough to squeeze into spaces and through tiny windows where they could not go taught him a lot. The only thing rigged around that door was the burglar alarm. One of the old-fashioned bell-ringing type, not even connected with the police station, and about as useful as Parkinson's disease. Another of Frankie's friends called earlier to deal with it, carrying an official-looking book and wearing a meter reader's hat. Twitchy day it had been, for the manager.

Two minutes, and the door yielded when the handle was turned. Jimmy signaled. The humpty-backed man picked up the two four-foot lengths of stout metal rail, which he had leaned against the alley wall, and scuttled across the deserted street.

Jimmy by now had the door open and was fixing the alarm system to look as though it was immobilized by the breaker-in. As it easily could have been, he was fully capable. But it takes a little time, and time spent fiddling in dark doorways with a guarded torch is high-risk time, and quite unnecessary if you can rig in advance. Make it look like a simple one-man break-and-enter, though, if you can. It cuts down lines of enquiry and is less likely to arouse wonder about the staff.

In through the door slipped humpty little Bertie. His lengths of metal chinked as the ends touched the jamb. "Keep it quiet, for Chrissake," hissed Jimmy. "You want the fucking pigs in?"

There was small danger of pigs, and they both knew it; but the flow of adrenaline—the wonderful, addictive heightening of all the senses, the heart-beating excitement—makes any sudden noise sound very, very loud in the up-tilted ears. The humpty man made no external reply; but because he was fifty-four years old and humpty, he hated all the slim, straight-bodied young who were neither. So in his head he said, Bollicks, as he passed on into the darkened shop.

Jimmy turned, the alarm rerigged (how is a trade secret, best kept in the family), adjusted his thin gloves, and moved to lead the way between racks of clothing—some little light here, glimmer from a street lamp—through a tarted-up wooden door in a sequinned wall (the manager also had flair for interior decoration) into a stockroom. Here he switched on his flashlight, heading for a further untarted door that led, he knew by his briefing, to the office where the safe would be.

Sure enough, there it was. Standing on a low support beyond the deal-wood desk, the filing cabinet and the normal clutter of a small office. Bertie moved forward, placing his lengths of steel to form a slide. This is all he was here for: to help maneuver the heavy, solid-looking safe away from the wall and onto the floor. Very strong arms and shoulders. A few muffled grunts, a little straining and the safe was off its support, down the slide and in position. Bertie removed the steel so that Jimmy could operate without hindrance on the back.

The back. There is the vulnerable part. Every policeman, every burglar knows that many of these antiquated, imposing safes, wrought mightily from thick, toughened steel on three sides, can be cut into through the back with a simple can opener.

A simple can opener is what Jimmy used, bought that day in Woolworth's. He would have preferred jelly—boys love an explosion—or to click the tumblers in time-honored fashion. He was very good at that and it gave deep satisfaction, he being young and keen enough still not to have arrived at blasé. But there's no doubt about it, a can opener does save time.

So he made the first jagged incision with a can opener. Then he handed this to Bertie, who gave him in exchange a pair of metal shears produced from a pocket; and with these he completed the job. Cut the whole damn back out. The way some people abuse their insurance policy is mortifying.

It is from ignorance, of course, in too many cases. Councillor

Mrs. Bagster, lying under the influence of whisky in a wide bed next to the wide bed containing her wealthy but snoring husband, had no idea that her safe and security system left anything to be desired. Nor did she know that at this very moment the safe was being opened up like a sardine tin.

For this, blame the man who came between her and natural sleep. Frankie had no intention that she should know. He elected her patsy on impulse, and for two reasons. Her junkie manager simplified the job so wonderfully; and it appealed to his sense of humor. Every time the police made contact, he believed, she would come nigh unto wetting herself, for fear they came bearing photographs. It enriched his little jest nicely, it thickened the cream for all those who would roll about holding their ribs, when he was gone and the photos were circulated between them and the police.

Once the back of the safe is out, nothing's to stop you dipping in. There were papers and a few books; but what Jimmy wanted was in a bag at the front and in three neat piles beside it: the day's take and a couple of bundles of new notes, straight from the bank. All of this money he was about to pocket; but Bertie stuck out the sort of hand that can crunch coconuts and said:

"Half."

"Not here, not here," said Jimmy. "We're not fucking about here—we'll split it later—"

"Half."

There was menace in the tone, and a menacing hunchback is a man not to be lightly regarded. Very bright Bertie was not, and even his mother never claimed it (died from drink, soon after release from Holloway); but he knew enough not to let his share vanish into Jimmy's pocket.

"Listen," said Jimmy. "We want to get away from here—"

"Half." One great gloved hand stuck out. The other balled into a fist.

"Oh, fuck," said Jimmy, and he split the day's take with the other man. This was their perk; Frankie had said they could keep it. Not bad, although it hadn't been one of the shop's busiest days. Unless perhaps the manager, knowing it was all going to vanish, kept a little for himself? Nearly two hundred pounds they got, in used notes and coin. Didn't take long, to count and divide it. Quite comfortable they were, for time.

Well, that was more or less it. Candy from a kid is much more difficult, as Jimmy could have testified, he having started that way in primary school. They simply left everything as it was and walked away. No need to reclaim the lengths of metal—you can buy a lot of metal with a hundred pounds, and it's foolish to walk about so burdened in the small hours.

So out they came again, through the stockroom and the shop. They didn't even bother to relock the front door. When the break-in was discovered did not matter a bit. Without a word of farewell, when they reached the street they melted away in opposite directions; Bertie to a mankey little room where he could gloat over what was, for him, a big payday; Jimmy by back streets to Rosher's garden, up over his little potting shed and in through a window, having in his possession the new notes, first plant in Rosher's house. No need even to notify Frankie that the job was done. When Frankie issued instructions, the job normally was done.

Three o'clock in the morning. Too late for a young and growing lad to be getting his head down. Later still, before he slept. The adrenaline flow does not cease the moment you leave the job.

Six hours later, a male not all that much older who had slept even less arrived at the shop, twitching. This was the manager; blue eyes, wavily blonded hair, beautiful maroon velvet slacks worn with a pretty jacket. Ernest Brownlow, twenty, whose friends called him Bibi. Had anybody been watching they might have noticed that he showed no surprise at finding the front door unlocked, and that he appeared to have a touch of the shakes. But nobody was watching. In that street at ten to nine in the morning, there is no time to stand and stare.

In he went, following the path Jimmy and Bertie had trod through shop and storeroom, into the office. There was the safe, standing on the floor with its back lying jagged-edged beside two lengths of flat metal rail. He barely glanced. What interested him, what alone had power to stop his shakes and strengthen him against the thing he had done and the things he must do, was in a little envelope he would find, the voice on the telephone had told him, tucked away inside his desk drawer. His supplier had been instructed yesterday: No more until the job is done.

By nine o'clock, when his staff arrived—two girls was the whole of it, and they treated him as a sister rather as manager—the twitch had stopped, the cheese color gone from his skin so that the teeny, teeny touch of rouge blended better, and his beautiful eyes were bright. He cried in his normal tone as they twittered around in their boutique baubles, over the moon with excitement:

"Don't touch anything, dears—for heaven's sake, don't touch anything. You know what the fuzzy-wuzzy is—they'll be trolling in and dusting everything for fingerprinties. I must ring Mrs. Bagster. No, no—don't touch it, Debbie—you'll get yourself arrested."

Councillor Mrs. Bagster was donning the great bra that kept her tremendous mammalian equipment within human tailoring when the call came to her bedside telephone, shrilling into her hangover. All calls were switched through at night, from the phone downstairs. "Hallo, Mrs. Bee," the machine cried in her wincing ear. "We've been robbed."

"Robbed?" said the councillor. The long lashes of her fine eyes moved tentatively up and down, to see if the lids were still lined with sandpaper. "Who's been robbed?"

"We have, dear," cried her manager. "We've been robbed. Henshawe Street. The safe—the back wall cut. Right out. All yesterday's take was in it. And the money I drew for the wages." His, the two girls', the cleaning lady's.

"Have you rung the police?"

"No!" He sounded quite shocked. "No, dear—I wouldn't do that until I'd told you."

"Better do it straightaway," said Councillor Mrs. Bagster. God knew, she wanted no dealings with the police; it jellied her when she had to meet the Chief Constable at social gatherings. She tended, even, to smile too brightly at the common or garden bobby on duty outside the town hall. Always one there, directing traffic. But what can one do? "I'll be right down."

"All rightee. By-eeee." In spite of the massive dose he had just pumped into himself, the manager's lovely limp-wristed hands shook when he put the telephone down and his palms were clammy with sweat. Private behind his office door, the girls twittering still in the now open-for-business shop—salon, they called it—he wiped them dry on a lace-edged handkerchief before he picked up the instrument again and dialed 999.

5

Detective Sergeant Rosher left his house this morning in a mood not far from cheerful. Too much to expect that he would whistle and sing, or even consider doing so; but very definitely, he knew a lightening of his mental and spiritual load, and his feet seemed not so heavy.

Food had a good deal to do with it, of course. Mental stress and depression create a vicious circle. Appetite goes; and the victim, left to look after himself, eats less and less of all the near food that is snatched from supermarkets and brought into the light of day by tin opener or out of a plastic package. They starve all the little nerves that should feed body and brain, these horrible travesties of honest food, and so create further stress and deeper depression.

In theory, as a one-time highly regarded amateur champion boxer, Rosher knew the value of food to the body, even if he had never considered it (or anything else, very much) in relation to the brain. Brain had never been his thing. In practice, he had neglected proper eating since his fall—he couldn't be bothered with it; and malnutrition starts in just that way.

Now, he was feeding. Every day he left for work with his belly, which until his fat wife left was threatening to paunch (that much good a baked bean diet did him, the little pot was gone), filled and highly gratified by solid nourishment, beautifully cooked and served, ravishing nostrils even before belly with that most glorious of morning perfumes: fried bacon. Every lunchtime he drove home; and there was more food, something stewed or cut up cold with salad. And in the evening, the sweet savor of a pie, or a pudding, or a roast set him salivating all over again. Once that vicious circle is broken, the body sets up clamor.

And then there was the new experience of a new woman bringing comfort and peaceful order to his surroundings, unobtrusively ministering when he was in, restoring and maintaining while he was out. No fat wife's prattling to be endured—nothing but peace and carpet slippers and the soft ticking of the clock. Telly, of course, when desired. All, except possibly the last, very wonderful.

Last evening he actually enjoyed. Made strangely mellow by food and circumstance—a good thick steak, all the trimmings and a purely golden apple pie, eaten in peace—he realized that his new treasure and her quiet, well-behaved children were being deprived of their nightly television quotient, because he possessed only one set, and it was in here. So he tapped upon the door between the two sitting rooms, and waited for her invitation before he opened it. The girl-child was in one armchair, the boy was not here. The mother sat on the settee, winding a ball of wool.

"Ah," said Sergeant Rosher; and his brownstone, tombstone teeth showed in a smile. Now how long was it since they did that? "I was wondering if you'd care to watch the telly. There's a film on—Miriam Hopkins and Joan Crawford."

"That's very kind of you," replied Margaret; and sweetly, to the child: "Would you like to watch the television, Helen?"

"I'm going out," the girl said, promptly. She wasn't spending her time watching telly with this old nit.

"Ah," said Rosher, who had no ease in the presence of the

young. When forced into their company he had adopted towards them, always since he ceased to be one, a sort of jovial bullying (and not so jovial, if he had them on the rug), worn to mask increasing mistrust and dislike. The two that had come into his life could not be bullied; so he gave gruff greeting when they met and avoided them so far as he could; as they, in truth, avoided him, if from more mixed motives. Except when the child helped her mother with the serving of his food, he seldom saw them. Now he said: "Ah," and hovered in the doorway as though not sure how to get out again.

"With her brother," said Margaret, quickly. Wouldn't do, to have him believe she allowed a pretty little blonde child to wander in strange streets at night, all unprotected. Even summer streets have danger these days, long before the dark comes down. "He's found out about a Youth Club." A likely story. What, Jimmy Burt? In a Youth Club? A piranha fish among chub.

"Ah," Rosher said again; and with a sudden flourish of his handkerchief produced his Doomsday trump; tucked away; coughed, and scratched his balding. "That'll be St. Marks, no doubt."

"Yes," said Margaret, extemporizing. "Yes, I believe he said St. Marks." Even as she spoke she thought: the vicar—Reverend Pew—St. Marks in his bloody church. Now they'll *have* to join—he may be talking to Rosher. If the little bitch would only cooperate, I wouldn't have to grab everything out of the air.

"Uh-huh," went Rosher. He added: "Well—if you'd care to— er—"

"Thank you. I'd like to." Why not? Frankie is right this far: The closer we get, the less he'll be watching his back.

So Rosher enjoyed—and actually knew he was enjoying—a domestic evening shared with a rounded and comely woman who wore very discreet perfume and got up at the program's end, to reappear with cocoa and bread and cheese on a tray. He liked cocoa. And she thanked him very nicely, a very nice woman in every way.

"Any time," he said. "If I'm not here and there's something you want to watch, help yourself." Out of the crusted chrysalis of the old curmudgeonly Rosher, a new Rosher, poking a tentatively expansive head. Nourished into being by steak and cocoa. And loneliness.

He would have been less pleased with the evening had he known what happened upstairs. So, for that matter, would Margaret; not on moral grounds so much as because it showed clearly the unreliable quality of her helpers. The young, of course, are by decree of nature light-minded and given over entirely to their own pleasure rather than to stern duty, especially since they realized what bloody idiots they have been, listening to the old bastards all those centuries. And here, she had a right couple.

It was inevitable, given two such youngsters brought into sudden close proximity. When she knew that Sergeant Rosher would be well ensconced with Margaret in front of the television set, the girl went up the stairs; where in the bedroom allotted to her she undressed and put on a short toweling dressing gown, a present from the man who directed a recent blue movie. Then she went along Rosher's corridor to his tiny spare room, and pushed open the door without knocking. Inside she found Jimmy Burt, lying on his bed in his underpants, leafing through a girlie magazine and showing an erection already.

In two, three minutes they were at it, plunging and lunging on Rosher's truckle bed, gaining extra titillation by the fact of their both being under the age of consent and he a policeman, sitting downstairs all unknowing; and by a small savor of incest.

And so, before the aged movie had run its creaking course and had been eased back into the box very carefully, for fear it crumble to dust before the peak-time repeat on Sunday, offenses against a minor (or minors; only due process of law could determine who was guilty of what and against whom) had been committed under his roof. Also under that roof before the night was out—and literally only just under, since Jimmy stashed it in

59

the attic where the sergeant never went—was money from a burglary, report of which reached the police station just after Rosher did.

He had driven through town with his stomach purring and his mind still pleasantly colored by his quiet evening in the company of a comely woman. It is a truism, that the mind without friends, abandoned to lonely stress, will react disproportionately to small kindness. So he actually bared those brownstone teeth quite cheerfully as he came in through the main station entrance and said to the uniform sergeant writing in the Incidents Book within the old-fashioned, glass-windowed information booth:

"Nice morning, Barney."

Startled, the sergeant looked up. Barney Dancey, a lifetime in the force and still with clear blue eyes mirroring an untroubled soul. Such saintly men are rare. "Er—yes," he said. "Lovely." He told no lie, the weather was moving to heat wave. It trembled upon his lip, to add the other man's given name of Alf; but even he could not bring himself quite to it. He watched as Rosher went on his way to the CID room, and thought:

What's up with him? He never does more than grunt, these days. He hasn't called me Barney since the Old Man bust him down. He hasn't called anybody anything. And he's got some of the spring back in his walk. Doesn't look very much worse than he used to look, in the old days, when a case went sour on him; and that's better than he's looked for months. He turned away, to answer the sudden buzz of the intercom.

It was an Inspector John Barclay. "Who's in the CID room, Barney?" he asked. "Got a sergeant, have we?"

"Alf Rosher just went in, John." The Alf slipped out automatically from Sergeant Barney's lips. The only lips from which it would.

"Rosher. Hmm." A hesitation. No specific orders had ever been issued—overt discrimination, that would have been—but everybody knew the Old Man's mind with regard to Rosher. It happened that Inspector John Barclay was one of those who felt the old sod should either have been slung out altogether or given another whip-crack. So he said, after his hesitation: "All right—send him in, will you?" He rang off, a brisk man with many things on his mind.

Three minutes later Rosher rapped boxer's knuckles on the door and entered. "Morning," he said. "You wanted me?"

"Yes, Sergeant, yes," said Inspector Barclay. "Morning. Break-and-enter. Betty's Boutique—Councillor Mrs. Bagster's place in Henshawe Street." He handed across his desk the form upon which are noted time of call and such details concerned with the incoming case as are so far known. Address, method of entry, estimate of loss, and so on. "Just come in. Go and have a look at it, will you? Any cars free?"

"Couple on the forecourt, when I came in."

"Take one, and a driver. All right?"

"Right," said Rosher, and left the office with his mood further risen. Time away from that bloody desk and the hated typewriter. Given the luck of a lead or two warranting further investigation, possibly a good deal of it, spread over a couple of weeks. Provided it didn't blow up too big, so that they appointed a heavier rank to handle the field work. Passing the information desk on his way back to the CID room he said:

"Taking a car, Barney. Ring through for a driver, will you?"

"Yes. Sure," said Sergeant Barney. Everybody called him that.

"Somebody who knows how to change gear." Rosher moved on, through the door to the hooks where hung the outdoor gear of CID men.

Well, well, Sergeant Barney said to himself as he pressed the intercom button. So they've given him something to do at last. Marvelous, the difference it makes to a man. A jest. Well, well, well. Not a good one, but a jest nevertheless.

Roughly half an hour after the call came in at the station switchboard, accompanied by a young and sprightly uniform constable who had joined the force recently for adventure and would leave next week disillusioned and in search of better pay, Detective Sergeant Rosher trod into the dinky boutique almost on the more agitated heels of Councillor Mrs. Bagster, who had

61

thrown her enormous tweeds on and driven straight down as promised, in a fine clashing of gears and jerking away from traffic lights. She could drive well enough, but her mind was on other things. To the two pretty but overproduced girl assistants, he said:

"Mr. Brownlow. The manager. Is he here?"

"Who shall I say wants him?" one of the girls asked. All dewy and aflutter with excitement they were still, the pair of them. She asked the question only to hear the answer. Quite obvious who wants him, when one of the callers wears a black hat low on his sternly simian bullet head, and the other is in uniform; but from rare excitement, maximum satisfaction must be garnered.

"Police. Detective Sergeant Rosher." Off came the black hat, revealing in its classic glory the authentic short back and sides, marred only by a hole in the top.

"Yes. I'll tell him." Happy rounded eyes exchanging thrills with the happy round eyes of her colleague, the pretty thing waggled away. When she came back it was in company with one even prettier, to tastes bent that way. Willow-slender. Blue eyes, wavily blonded hair, beautiful maroon slacks worn with a pretty jacket. Hands sweaty. Or perhaps not sweaty. Much too gross. Hands delicately perspiring, and heart going pitty-pat.

"Good *morning!*" cried the manager, his lovely eyes batting lashes on general principle. At any other time he would doubtless have batted at the young, big, butch constable standing solid in blue serge—policemen get batted at quite often, sometimes by both subjects at the very time of arrest in public urinals—but he did it now without intent. It was not his day for batting at policemen.

"Good morning," said Sergeant Rosher; and added: "sir." The word came hard. He hated pooves. Aftershave was all right; but apart from this, a man should smell of honest sweat. And liniment, when he needs it.

"You're the *police*," the manager said.

"We are, sir." Rosher flashed his identity card. Who the bloody heck else would we be?

"It's in the *office*," said Ernest Brownlow, known to his friends as Bibi. "Would you like to see it?"

"If you please, yes." We didn't come to look at you, son, did we? Phoo—what are you wearing, Careless Rupture?

"This way." The manager turned to lead the way through the stockroom to the office, bum waggling. He did it quite as well as the two girls left twittering in the salon.

In the office stood the broken safe, and Councillor Mrs. Bagster. Over by the desk she was, all the great bolster bust of her, the square tweed and the thick legs that had but one circumference all the way down. Impenetrable disguise for a madly beating heart, that bolster bosom, and owners of such tweeds can hide trembling hands by thrusting them deep into the pockets. "Ah, good morning, Councillor," said Rosher, coming in.

"Good morning, Sergeant." Oh, a shock, to see him. Of all policemen! The very one whose hard little eyes and ape-shape haunted her onto last night's whisky. He and a laughing Irishman with a friend who took pictures. The one who would never be fooled for long by the people planted on him, who would be rooting even now into their background. What that background might be, she didn't know. Hadn't been told. But they must be crooked, to be mixed in with Daly. Better to have gone to the police, straightaway.

But it was done now—she hadn't been able to face her political and social destruction should the promise of privacy for blackmail victims leak, she had made in her mind hideous scenes where policemen tittered, poring over pictures of her naked with a whip, tits akimbo as she plied upon two bound and naked young ladies. So now, with quivering gut she forced a smile. It came very bright. "Here's a pretty kettle of fish," she said.

"Yes, madam," replied Sergeant Rosher. He wore the heavy, portentous look he always considered proper at the scene of a crime, and his mouth uttered scrupulous politeness. Stage one of his investigative technique, formed and kept well honed in the days when he had plenty to investigate. Rusty now, but you never lose it. Like riding a bicycle. "Let's have a look at things, shall we?"

An experienced policeman does not need close examination to establish that the thin back of an old safe has been cut out. He knows it before he looks at it; it happens all the time. Just as he knows that when a second car draws up outside a robbed boutique and two more plainclothes men enter, here come the Forensic boys, to dust around and waft away with their little bottles and bunny-puff brushes, and find nothing. Nobody but a complete idiot operates without gloves. Not in these days, when the training schools of cinema and television are free to all, and the fate of the Great Train Robbers still shudders in the memory. Thirty years, for a few fingerprints left in a farmhouse.

"Morning, gents," said Detective Sergeant Rosher, and nodded to the safe as they made reply. "Doubt if you'll find anything." The two Forensic men placed their small bags on the convenient desk and began to draw forth their equipment. Rosher addressed the councillor.

"Do you know what's missing, madam?"

"Er—," said Mrs. Bagster, hands still jammed into her jacket pockets. She looked at her manager, still with the oddly bright smile on her face. He answered for her.

"About two hundred *pounds*. The day's *take*. And *another* two hundred. I drew the wages—Debbie and Rosanna. And Mrs. Filton."

"Mrs. Filton?"

"The cleaning lady. And *me*— my salary was there."

"New notes?"

The heart in the willowy chest or breast beat up against its shield of dope. "Yes. I went to the bank yesterday."

"What bank would that be, sir?"

"Barclays. Why? Does it matter?"

This was a question prompted by fear. Simple matter, for the police to find out from the bank that never before had he asked specifically for new notes, when he cashed the salary check. The policeman was eyeing him keenly. Not knowing that Rosher, engaged on investigation, eyed everybody keenly just because he felt one should, he almost confessed there and then. But Rosher merely said: "No, sir. Just one of the details we like to have filled in. Do you always draw the salaries a day in advance?"

Again Mrs. Bagster looked expectantly at the lad. Obviously, day-to-day running of her branches was left very much to her managers. Well, that's the secret of success, know how to delegate. But it also opens the way to funny business.

"Not *always*," said Bibi. "Sometimes I do. It depends."

"What on?"

Rosher's keen eye, his portentous look, his sternly abrupt questions, even the way he held that *terrible* black hat between hairy hands were shooting the manager's nerves to pieces. Combine such a personality with the silent bulk of a second policeman, uniformed, standing solid in the background (only he knowing he was leaving next week, to tighten nuts on car bodies in Coventry) while two more of the ilk begin to dust a rifled safe, and there is nothing soothy in the situation even for the innocent. So intent was Bibi upon keeping a quiver out of his voice, he quite forgot his usual camp emphases.

"Well, whether I think I'll be able to get to the bank on Friday. We're having a sale next week—aren't we, Mrs. B.?—all those tickets to make out."

"Uh-huh." The sergeant indicated the safe. "You leave it overnight in that? Together with the day's takings?"

"Yes. It's—it's always been all right before."

How many times had he heard that? The sergeant addressed the bolster-bosomed lady. "Not altogether wise, madam, in view of the vulnerability. Did you install the safe?

If Councillor Mrs. Bagster had remained dumb so far, it was partly because she feared a gargle if she tried to speak. Forced to it now, she moved her lips. What came out sounded not too bad. She had reason for showing a little upset, as owner of a robbed boutique. As did the manager, here with a boss who might hold him responsible, even if she did not suspect how. "No, it was in when I took the place over. Two years ago."

"Uh-huh. Have you ever seen the back?"

"No. No, it's always stood there—against the wall."

"Uh-hnn." Much of what Rosher was saying now had no special significance. He'd been through it all a dozen times, with the victims who had put their trust in these old boxes. But it made a show, while he waited for the fingerprint men to find their nothing. He carried on.

"And the alarm system. That was here, too?"

"Yes. It seemed to work all right." The councillor took her hands out of her pockets; felt their clammy trembling and hid them behind her back, with a smile brighter yet.

"Easily jammed, these old bell systems. Might be wise to overhaul the entire security system. We can advise you, if you'd care to contact us at the station." If all her branches were similarly served, there could be a nice penny in it for a firm re-equipping them all on contract. Not that he, or any other copper, would benefit; except, perhaps, in lessened work load. Half the small shops in the town gave open invitation to every competent burglar who flicked an eye around as he bought a packet of wine-gums or pipe cleaners. Too many accepted gratefully; and the paper piled up on CID desks.

"Yes," she said. "Yes. I'll call in." But greater fears she had than burglary of shops all covered by insurance.

"The new notes," said Rosher. "Did you take the numbers?"

Once more she moved the fine eyes to Bibi. Once more he answered: "Yes. Yes, I—they're in my desk drawer."

Well, that's something, Rosher thought. Half the bloody fools don't even do that. The poove's making for the desk. "Hold on a minute, sir." To the fingerprint men: "All right, to open the desk drawer?"

One of the men looked up from his dusting. "So long as you don't touch it."

"I'll do it for you, sir," said Rosher, and opened the drawer by means of a pencil behind the handle, pulled both ends. Bibi drew out and handed to him a small paper upon which the note numbers appeared written neatly under two headings, £5 and £10. "Thank you very much," Rosher said, and began to copy them into his notebook. The man who spoke for the forensic workers made his initial report.

"Nothing here, so far as we can see."

"Uh-huh," answered Rosher, knowing the speech to be not much more than formality. The fingerprint men had known there would be nothing, as surely as he did himself. There'd be nothing on the front door, too—the manager, the two girls, the councillor had all come in that way before he got here, thus obliterating anything that might have been. Which was nothing. He said to the councillor:

"Perhaps we can go into the other room, madam, while these gentlemen get on." They'd have to do the lot—desk, filing cabinet, and so on. And not only for fingerprints. Looking for fibers, looking for anything.

"Yes. Yes, of course." The councillor set her tweed in motion, leading the manager, the sergeant, and his silent acolyte out into the stockroom. The forensic men dusted on.

Twenty minutes later all the policemen left, Rosher assuring Mrs. Bagster that everything that could be done would be done. And that's not much, he thought. An ear to the ground—listen and ask questions. No solid leads. Unless somebody murmuring speaks it, not much hope in this day of chronic undermanning. Too many similar jobs for every one to get full attention. In the salon on the way out, he said:

"Your Mrs. Loving and the children. They seem to be settling in quite well."

The councillor's cushioned heart gave a tremendous bound. Not my Mrs. Loving—Frank Daly's Mrs. Loving. "Oh, good," she said enthusiastically. Her beam was a credit to the maker, an old-fashioned craftsman still mourning the passing of pottery teeth, in the creation of which a man could take proper pride. "Good. I'm so glad."

"Pleasant woman. Very competent. Well, we'll be in touch, as soon as we have news for you. Good morning, Councillor." He donned his black hat in order to doff it, settled it back on his head again, well down over his ears; nodded to the poove.

"Good morning, Sergeant," said Councillor Mrs. Bagster. "Thank you very much." And the Sergeant took himself away, leaving two beating hearts, two churning stomachs, two secret minds giving thanks for this small mercy, four palms being surreptitiously wiped dry of sweat; two souls wishing: one—oh, for the millionth time—that she had never heard of girls or whips; the other, that she would sod off, so that he could nip into the bog for a teensy, weensy fix. Both too cut off in their own fear to take a good look at the other.

Rosher, on the other hand, found that the episode had added fresh depth to his sense of well-being. It felt good, to be in the field again, almost as if he had never been away. He drove the car back to the station with the driver-constable sitting beside him, enjoying the renewed pleasure of all that power under his foot, so much livelier and more responsive than anything he could afford in his own car. It was not often, these days, that he got the chance to drive an official car. And never since the fall had he whacked the typewriter with zest, as he did when he regained his desk to make his preliminary report. To Inspector John Barclay only. Break-and-enter jobs are much too common for every one to go upstairs.

This one *might* rise to Superintendent level, because of the name of the victim. Local politicians can rant against the police at meetings reported in newspapers, if their property is not smartly recovered; but some sort of self-protection is afforded if a high-ranking policeman in charge of the case can refer snidely to antediluvian security systems. Most likely it would remain exactly as it was: a petty crime handled in the field by a sergeant and perhaps a constable, with an inspector at home to carry the top weight.

So Rosher typed his report and took it in to Inspector John Barclay, who glanced through it and said:

"Uh-huh. Usual pattern? Nothing to go on?"

"Not a thing," said Rosher. "I'll do a bit of nosing around. The manager's queer—I'll take a look at the Green Baytree." Town center club, where all the queers gathered. You never know, with shops—it might be an inside job. It would make an outing, anyway.

"Right." The inspector put the report into his tray; pondered a moment the problem of whether he should hand the job on to some other sergeant; picked up the paper he had been studying. "Let me know, if anything turns up." Give the poor old sod a chance.

Most profitable hunting time for detectives is evening, when people gather into pubs and clubs. Rosher looked in to some of the dubious during the lunchtime session, but more for the pleasure of being back in harness than from hope. The little people seemed surprised to see him, because of late he had neglected his old contacts, knowing himself to be laughingstock among them. A laughingstock has no teeth, and so his carefully nurtured circle of whispering men broke and vanished like a fairy ring overnight. Unlikely, that he could ever rebuild. When he left them now they would titter together, he knew; but somehow, the knowledge destroyed him less.

In the afternoon he rang Margaret, to ask for an early dinner so that he could be out and about again, extracting all the pleasure while he could. Maybe—maybe they were going to let him off the chain sometimes, from now. Maybe he had served his unofficial sentence, perhaps the Old Man was at last putting him back to what he was good at. What with the manpower shortage and everything—that lad who came with him this morning was off into a factory, the daft young bugger—good detectives were not to be wasted.

"Yes'" said the soft woman's voice. "I can do that. About what time?"

"Say, five thirty?" Odd time for dinner, but seasoned coppers fill up while the chance is offered.

"I'll see that it's ready."

What a difference it makes, the sergeant thought, to have a woman backing you. In a sudden wave of gratitude and near affection—the two conditions so closely related—he said:

"I may be out pretty late—if there's anything you want to watch on the telly, don't hesitate."

"Thank you," she said. "You're very kind."

"Not at all, not at all. See you later, then."

The near affection continued after he put the phone down. A pleasant feeling, part of a pleasant day. What I should really do, he thought under the influence of it, is get another set. Hire one—put it in the other room.

To Rosher's mind, obviously, the trial period was over. In his newfound enthusiasm for domestic comfort and appreciation of its source, he rode right over his famed tightfistedness. Anyway, he told himself now when it reared an alarmed head, she's working cheap. Mind you, I haven't yet had the butcher's bills and grocery bills, and if they're all eating as well as I am—. He pushed the thought down, and took a new one. His fat wife *always* ate enough for four. And prattled while she did.

By six o'clock he was gloriously fed again, so comfortably fullbellied that he almost regretted having to do what he had looked forward to: get up and go, to the seedy world of pub and club. It would have been nice, to repeat the pleasure of yesterday evening. There was never much on the box, of a Friday; but comely, quiet company can render even Coronation Street tolerable. All the good protein rich inside him, soothing his mind as it cherished his body, in a new wave of gratitude he said to the mother as her daughter removed his rhubarb tart plate:

"Yes—the telly. Help yourself, don't stand on ceremony."

"Thank you." She placed before him cream crackers, water biscuits, three kinds of cheese, all on a wooden board. Black eye faded to a faint discoloration now, abrasions nearly gone. She was phasing them out.

"Ah," he said. "Cheese. Yes—always a good finish, cheese. Yes—as a matter of fact, I was thinking I'd better get another set in. Hire one."

"Will we be staying on, then?"

"Well—. Hmm. Hrummph. I'm perfectly satisfied, if you are. Perfectly."

"Oh, yes—we're—thank you. You are very kind."

"Right. Good. Yes. Well, then—perhaps you'd like to fix it, when you're out shopping. Tomorrow. There's a Rediffusion place in town; if you bring the forms I'll sign 'em. Don't stint yourself—get color."

His own set was black and white. Quite good enough, for a man who cut his entertainment teeth on Buster Keaton and Lillian Gish, in the days when movies had captions; but gratitude and a full belly do inspire affection, and with it the need to give nobly. A young woman, and children especially, they need color. Give it to her, then, let her see you appreciate. You may regret it later, but it's a poor heart that never rejoices.

"Oh," she said. "Thank you." And she repeated: "You're very kind." By now, playing the part smoothly.

"Not at all, not at all." Rosher bared the brownstone teeth; made a small, surreptitious burp, and reached for the cheese. With his mouth full, he spoke again. "This case I'm on—it may interest you. Councillor Mrs. Bagster—one of her shops broken into. They've put me in charge." When a man comes to even partial resurrection, he needs to pass the good news on. Normally, lacking wider audience, he will commandeer the ear of a woman living in his house.

"Really? How interesting." Immediately, she knew what Jimmy had not told her: whence came the new notes just stashed in the house. A ripple of alarm touched her. Obviously, Frankie had something on this councillor woman; quite as obviously, to embroil her willy-nilly in his little joke would appeal to his sense of humor; but unnecessarily risky, to invite more than normally thorough investigation by burgling a public figure. "Do you think you'll catch whoever did it?" she asked.

It pleased him, this question. He liked a woman to be The Little Woman, very little better than an admiring halfwit. "Not much to go on," he said. "But I shall try. You may depend on

71

that." He bared his teeth again. Frightening. Some of the gorilla ferocity was back in it. All show, of course, for a woman's sake. As it is, at least come springtime, in gorillas. Not much more chance of his closing the case than there is of the gorilla mating with a rhesus monkey.

Half an hour later, when he was gone, she telephoned Frankie. "Hallo, darling," his beautiful voice said. "How are you getting on?"

"Quite well, I think. Your friend is waiving the two-week trial. Says he's perfectly satisfied."

"Good. Very good. You know your lad's been at work, don't you?"

"Yes."

"I'm well pleased with him, he operated very nicely. I'll be back to you on that." By the way he spoke, you'd have thought the boy really was her son.

"Right." And because a woman also likes to confide her little triumphs: "Your ape-man is going to rent us a telly."

"Is he?" Frankie laughed. "Who from?"

"He's told me to get the forms from Rediffusion, when I go shopping tomorrow."

Frankie's quick mind immediately saw further opportunity. "Go in the morning—get the forms. Have him sign them, and you keep 'em. Burn them—doesn't matter. Leave the rest to me."

"Why?"

"You'll see, darling—you'll see. Anything else?"

"No. Yes—do you know anything about a boutique being done?"

Frankie's turn to say: "Why?"

"Because your friend's been put in charge."

At the other end of the line, the man fell about in uproarious mirth. In attendance as usual, Jokey Fenton said unsmiling:

"What's funny?"

"I'll tell you in a minute," Frankie spluttered. The phone was squawking again in his ear. Tears on his cheeks, all alight with joy, he controlled his voice enough to ask: "What was that, darling? Didn't catch it."

72

"I said: Don't overdo it, for Chrissake."

"Don't you worry your pretty head, darling. Don't you worry about a thing." Laughing still, as he would for some time, Frankie hung up. Margaret replaced the phone, frowning. She didn't like this, very much. The bastard's right hand, at all times, ought to know what the bastard's left hand is stirring.

It was a reckless thing to do, of course. Irish equals reckless. As a matter of record, although he didn't know it, Rosher came red-hot close to the heart of the matter later that evening. He'd called in pubs, he'd called at clubs, and come up with nothing. Which did not bother him, it was just as expected. Shortly before closing time he looked into the Green Man in Fowler Street, where many small crooks drink, when they have the price of a pint or hope that somebody who has will stand them one; and as he went toward the bar, a squat man carrying two double-measure shorts turned and bumped into him.

"Watch it, watch it," he advised, as he reached to steady the teetering shoulders. Pissed as a newt, he thought.

"Watch it yourself, mate," snapped the humpty-backed man, and wobbled on his way. Bertie Smithers, out spending his big payday with a poor, bedraggled whore. A man unknown to Rosher come to this town only recently when a move from Sutton Coldfield seemed advisable. Once, feared and hated as Old Blubbergut, the copper would have heard about him on the very day of his arrival; but Old Blubbergut, now dubbed the Bicycle King, had been chained to his desk for months. So he drank half a pint of bitter, looked the place over with his hard eyes, some of the talk dying as he did so, and left. Bertie went on with his drinking, which would not have pleased Frankie, had he known. Even when the whore, the one person who loved him (when he had money), told him who it was he'd bumped into, he didn't care a monkey's. Whisky and natural stupidity, in solution, combine to make a man gloriously invulnerable. They also make him randy. Not that Bertie needed help with this. Poor bugger, he didn't get a lot. Hadn't often got money.

6

The man with his ear open to catch Frankie Daly's phone calls, going in or out, thought highly enough of this one to send the transcription and cassette, sealed, straight in to young Inspector Cruse, still in his office clearing up a report on an unrelated case. Inspector Cruse was sufficiently impressed by it to pick up his hat at once and make for a public booth, thus bypassing the station switchboard. It cut down the chance of leakage. When the dial had been manipulated and the phone had buzzed and been answered, he put in his money, exchanged identities and said:

"Sorry to bother you this time in the evening, sir."

"Quite all right, Inspector," the Chief Constable said. "So long as the matter is urgent."

"Thought you ought to hear this right away." Even if it buggers your dinner up. A cough, to clear the throat; and Cruse read the transcript. The Chief listened in silence through to the end. This reached:

"Mm. Interesting. Very interesting," he said. "Read it again."

Cruse did so. As he came toward the finish, the phone blip-blipped. He fumbled another twopenny piece into the slot; com-

74

pleted his recital; said: "That's my last two pee."

"Number?" the Chief commanded and when he had it: "Hang up—I'll ring back." Nice and private, public 'phone booths, but all the fiddling about can be most off-putting.

Inspector Cruse stood with the receiver pressed onto its stand. As soon as the ringing came, he picked the thing up and clapped it to his ear, still warm from the last time. "What do you make of it?" his chief said at once, without even asking if it was indeed he.

"Well, sir, it's a bit obscure, but it seems to suggest that some of Daly's friends are in close contact with a member of the force."

"It doesn't say anything about a member of the force."

Typical top-brass rejoiner. With the possibility of a bent copper already in mind, each saw well enough what was implied. But top brass likes to be seen functioning as controlling curb on the impetuosity of junior rank. Furbishes the image. Cruse said: "It seems to suggest it, though, sir. 'Your friend's been put in charge.'"

"Mm. Rrmph. Not necessarily—the feller who did the transcript could have made a mistake. It could have said your friend's been taken in charge."

"Yes, sir." Except that the same phrase spoke very clearly out of the cassette. But soft answer, no wrath. "It could. We can check against the tape. Anyway, it seems to connect Daly with a boutique being done."

"Not even that, really. What boutique?" Not usual, for the Chief to be so obtuse. Perhaps he had dinner guests listening, waiting to be impressed.

"I don't know, sir, but I'll soon find out." No disgrace in admitting to ignorance. The keenest policeman cannot be expected, even by a barking Chief Constable, to be *au fait* with every petty crime on the station books. Certainly not in this day and age.

"Do that. And check who's in charge. Ring me back, if the thing seems to warrant it."

Very soon after, back at the station, Cruse had found Betty's Boutique written into the book, with Detective Sergeant Rosher handling the legwork; who is, to all intents and purposes, in charge, even though authority for anything more than routine action must come (in theory) from the senior rank whose name appears at the top of the file.

Out he went again to the phone, with no twopenny piece at all this time and no intention of blowing cover by tapping around. Instead, he dialed the Chief's number, let it ring for a short time, and hung up. In a small minute the instrument shrilled. "Cruse?" said the Chief Constable. "Thought it'd be you. Remembered you had no two pee pieces." Lightning, the trained mind. Looked at the number noted on the pad and dialed it instantaneously. As the other feller knew he would. "Get anything?"

"The boutique, sir. Betty's Boutique is the only one we have record of. Proprietor, Councillor Mrs. Bagster. John Barclay has it. Sergeant Rosher is handling it. No arrest."

"Ah." Rosher? Rosher should be chained to a desk. "Councillor Mrs. Bagster, eh? Report in yet, from Rosher?"

"Only the preliminary, in the file. Safe cut into—about £400 gone, two hundred in new fives and tens, numbers noted. Forensic report's there, too, of course. Negative."

"Uh-huh." What's Barclay thinking about, putting Rosher onto it? "We'd better contact Inspector Barclay. I'll be down. No—wait. The Dun Cow, on the bypass. I'll be there in fifteen minutes." Starts a station murmuring, when a Chief Constable returns to it late in an evening and closets himself with an inspector. Besides, Barclay might be the bent.

Fifteen minutes later young Inspector Cruse arrived at the Dun Cow, entering through a door tricked out as Tudor and set into a façade magpied with white paint and nailed-on beams, to an interior of horse-brassy glass-fiber rusticity. Only two drinkers here, one of whom was gloomily inserting money into a jukebox standing in a Tudor fireplace lurid with cheap new brick. It clicked as Cruse came in and began to cacophonate a rock arrangement of "Greensleeves."

No Chief Constable, as yet. He crossed woodblock flooring to the Instant Tudor bar and ordered a pint of bitter, from a barmaid of the type many thousands of ages old when Shakespeare was a lad. She fluttered her long tacky lashes at him, simpering under a high nest of black, black hair because he was a good-looking young man, with the muscles bar ladies love; saying as she served him:

"There we are, dear. First today, eh? Haven't seen you in here before, have we?"

"Thank you," he said. "No. Just out for a drive, thought I'd drop in. Very fond of Tudor pubs."

"Ain't we all?" She widened her simper, polishing a glass so enthusiastically that what Shakespeare called the paps jumped gently up and down. It pays to advertise. "I don't think it is Tudor, though, reely."

"Isn't it?" He took the first, satisfying pull at his pint. Tasted fine, to him. Men so young never met the firm, full flavor of real beer.

"No. I think they built it when they built the bypass. I *think* they did, but I haven't been here long. Used to work at the Kings Head. In Blaydon Road. Do you know it?"

"Yes," he said, frankly enjoying the feminine joggle. "Do you like it better here?"

"Oh, *yes!*" She patted her hair; set the glass aside; picked up another, and started herself jumping again. "So much more character."

Now, just when his smile encouraged her to polish glasses as never before—this wasn't a pub where the men wore many muscles—the Chief Constable came in; looking, Cruse thought, more Roman-headed and bull-shouldered in these prettied surroundings than was strictly necessary. Strangely, he bulked larger here than when seated at his desk, even though the seated position disguised the fact that his legs were inadequate for the

77

upper frame and massive head, the knees having a tendency to knock. The young man rose from his stool at the bar, saying:

"Good evening, sir. What'll you have?"

"Good evening, good evening," said the Chief Constable. "In the chair, are you? I'll take a double scotch."

I thought you bloody would, Cruse thought. He looked to the barmaid, dividing her eye-play now between no fewer than two men with muscles. One was old enough to be her father, but still. . . . That didn't mean he couldn't raise a gallop. "Double scotch, dear," she said. "Coming right up." Should she add her funny, "as the bishop said to the organist's wife"? Perhaps not. You never quite know, with men. Except commercials. And these were not commercials; they didn't have the leery look. The old one hadn't so much as glanced at her tits, not once.

They took their drinks to a table private in a corner. "Greensleeves" died on the jukebox with another small click. The devotee inserted more money. It began to roar a second platter of rock, this one abandoning all pretense at being Tudor. "Bloody racket," the Chief Constable growled. "Don't know what pubs are coming to. People used to play darts. Dominoes. Well, now—Rosher, do you think?"

"Looks a bit odd, sir, doesn't it?"

"Mm. Hmm." They sat awhile, in thought. When the leader thinks, subordinate flesh can but follow.

It had been in the Chief Constable's mind to have Rosher taken off the case. By his unspoken edict, Rosher dealt in paper. But, if the man was bent and dealing with Daly, better have him out and about, see whom he meets, where he goes, what sort of social life he is leading.

"Put a tail on him," he said at last. "And Alec—put one on Barclay, too." Barclay put Rosher in charge. More than one bent, acting in cahoots? Though why he should hand the job over to Rosher, or why Rosher would want it—who was to say? Strange are the ways.

"Will do, sir," Cruse promised; and very soon they went their ways. To the disappointment of the barmaid, who said, "Come again." There was nobody left now worth polishing a glass for.

Rosher, then, was under surveillance from the time he drove into his street after a fruitless but personally gratifying evening among the shadier watering holes. Perhaps some of his restoring vigor showed in him already, or maybe he was rendered less morbidly sensitive to mockery by good food and the sense of well-being. Whatever the reason, most of his old contacts seemed to react to his second birth with decent respect, outwardly at least. One who did not got barked at. It had been quite like old times. And more, perhaps, to come. He left his car standing in his short drive, noted approvingly that somebody had weeded the flowerbeds, and entered his kingdom content, all unaware of a thickset gent on the opposite side of the road who took care to keep him ignorant by hiding behind a bush.

The tail on Inspector Barclay came off almost before it went on, when a first report from the man behind the bush told, even before the Sergeant got home, of people living in his house. A woman, who switched lights on and drew curtains; a young girl, who came in soon after dark; and later, with Rosher long inside and all the lights out, a boy who moved carefully up the dark drive and went round the side of the house, presumably to enter through a window, since he didn't come out again. Damn it, the Chief Constable said to himself when he considered the matter, I've known John Barclay thirty years. You can't tail every man in the station; you'd have to put tails on the tails. And so, *ad infinitum*. Nothing in John Barclay's house but a pregnant wife and a testy mother.

By the following morning—it was Saturday—the watch upon Rosher's house had moved under cover of scrubland bushes and darkness into a convenient barn set back from the road. Nobody ever came here, not even children. They said it was haunted, by the old man who hanged himself in it. The hidden watchers, prepared to stiffen the belief with hollow groans and chokings, were able to report sundry things, and to prove their veracity with pictures taken by a bald-headed copper on a camera with a telephoto lens. A bent policeman is a grave encumbrance. The Chief Constable meant to know who these people were.

The pictures. First there was Rosher, leaving for work: black hat riding low, face a little screwed because he was flicking a fly from his nose when the shutter fell; but undoubtedly Rosher, battleship gray raincoat over his arm—not needed, this sunny July morning, but by noon in these latitudes you could be in a snow storm—off to do his duty with another fine breakfast inside him.

Then came Margaret; half an hour later, away to the shops with a basket over her arm. Rosher's fat wife bought that basket and carried it around the town, wheezing, for many years. Now it left the house with Margaret and the camera caught her with it, walking down the garden path looking plump as a comely chicken and very much more toothsome than anything she might prod in the supermarket. A very good shot, this one, well worth an eight-by-six enlargement and half a dozen postcards. Background perspective a little looming, as in any photograph taken with a telephoto lens; but this picture would never grace a sideboard. It was strictly a matter between the Chief Constable, Inspector Alec Cruse, and the picked men of the watch, chosen as being not inclined to prattle.

The next shot was of an upstairs window, open to this warm morning. Inside, what looked like the young girl naked in the naked arms of the lad reported last night as entering through a back window. Not very clear, this one. It is difficult to obtain an accurate light-meter reading into a shadowed interior, across sunlight, from a barn seventy yards away.

Shot number four. This was of the girl, demure now with plaited blonde hair and wearing the jeans and bright top ubiquitous among the young, leaving the house about some business of her own. Policemen are not made from sheet asbestos; they are constructed mind and body as other men; and the bald photographer felt a certain stirring as he ranged in on her, at memory of the last time he trained his lens upon her, beyond the open window in the arms of the lucky lad; who appeared in picture five, also clad in jeans and a tee shirt, yellow with OHIO UNIVERSITY lettered across it; also off on his own affairs.

Shot number six, taken after Margaret returned home from shopping and Rosher had come at one o'clock and departed again at two, filled with lunch—happenings not recorded by the camera, being extraneous to the job of identification. Shot number six was interesting. The second plant, going in.

It showed, all too close together and with the relative sizes of the people all wrong—again, perspective-distortion due to the telephoto lens—Margaret at the open door, watching as two men in flat caps carried a television set up the drive from a plain van in the foreground, parked on the road in front of the gate. One man had his back to the camera; but the other came out very nicely, in full face, with the set look that comes when the face owner is manhandling something heavy. By the miracle of fine-grain film and meticulously ground optics, the sweat could almost be seen. This point was seized upon by young Inspector Cruse when he studied the photographs, wet still from their final rinsing, in the Chief Constable's office.

"You can almost see the sweat," he said.

The Chief Constable grunted. He was not interested in technological brilliance except insofar as it assisted with the job of criminal investigation, apprehension, and clapping behind bars. With the six big prints spread over a large sheet of blotting paper on his desk, he said:

"Recognize any of these people?"

"Only him." Cruse pointed to the full-face man in the flat hat. "Eddie Greenwood. Specializes in belting O.A.P.'s for their pensions. Robbery with violence, that's Eddie. Likes to belt people. If that's a hump on the other one's back, he could be Bertie Smithers."

"Connection with Daly?"

"I don't know of any, sir. But they're mostly on tap when needed, aren't they, these little people? I'll have it looked at."

"Discreetly. Very discreetly. We don't want to blow this job coming up."

"Yes, sir." You do say some bloody silly things, sometimes.

Not likely to walk up hollering, Oy—how do you tie up with Mad Frankie Daly. Am I?

"What about the others?" the Chief was saying.

"Don't recognize them, sir. From out of town, presumably. Something to do with the big job? They're not local. Perhaps he's simply hired a housekeeper—he's all on his own up there."

"Very funny housekeeping." The Chief indicated the picture taken through the open window.

"Yes, sir," said Cruse. Incest, if they were a family. And if they were not, what were they?

The Chief pointed to the wet prints. "Get 'em blown up and circulated. Let me know at once, if anything turns up. And if Rosher leaves the station, have a man on his back."

"Yes, sir." But that's not so easy, mate. The old bugger knows every wart on every man in the station. Policewoman, perhaps. Summertime dress and a pretty hat. That's if we can find one who wouldn't look like the Mighty Hackenshmidt in drag.

In the event, no personal tail was put on Rosher that day. Second thoughts prevailed. It would have been necessary to call for assistance to men from other stations far away; and the tailing of a policeman by policemen is tempting as matter for conversation, when the man detailed as tail is back on home ground. So Rosher spent a pleasant morning, knocking up from out of their beds little men known to specialize in small burglaries, to eliminate them from a list; or to put a tick beside the name of a man who had no firm alibi and could not remember where he was while Mrs. Bagster's shop was being done. He left a good deal of cursing agitation in his wake. No night worker likes being woken up in the morning, and many of these were out and about at the time in question. Since he did not reveal which particular case he was working at, they all believed the bastard was on to them. This unsettles the nerves. Burglary is a profession shot through with nervous apprehension. By the time he drove home for lunch, so coming again under the eye of the watch still in the barn, Inspector Cruse had been to see Councillor Mrs. Bagster.

82

This was Cruse's own idea. Back in his office and giving the matter his full attention, he thought: Why just this one shop? Back he went, up the stairs again to the Chief Constable's office; and when he was standing in front of the big mahogany desk— higher the rank, better the wood—he said:

"I was wondering, sir—why just that one shop?"

"Uh-huh." The Chief Constable answered noncomittally. Top brass never admits that its eagle eye has not scanned the entire terrain. It grunts encouragingly, and waits for junior rank to elaborate. During the listening time it can then frame reply that suggests the point was long ago spotted, and well done, lad, for getting there in the end. As we all knew you would. "Carry on."

"Well, there are shops right along Henshawe Street. Normal pattern is to do several at once, isn't it?"

"Perhaps the others have better alarm systems." The Chief spoke not as though the thought was original to the moment, but rather as the parent or teacher speaks who knows the answer, and is holding down approval while the youngster gets it right.

"About half of em, sir, if it runs to average. We can soon check. Usual thing is to do the easy ones and leave the rest alone. So why this particular one?"

The Chief had the drift of it now. He nodded the massive nod, smiled the little smile that from him was a pat on the head. Said again: "Uh-huh." And waited, elbows on desk, fingers steepled.

"Four hundred quid, and half of that in traceable new notes. What's Daly doing, mucking about with peanuts like that?"

In full cry, the Chief's mind now. "Unless it's a cover. May have been something else there he wanted. Took the money as a blind."

"By the report, nothing else was taken."

"Mm. Yes." The Chief sat and thought for a moment, all the gears meshing in his noble head. Then he said: "Are you busy?"

"Nothing I can't drop, sir."

"Take an hour—go along and see Mrs. Bagster. Better ring to say you're coming, don't just barge in." Or waste time knocking on the door of an empty house. "See what you can pick up; there may have been something in the safe she's forgotten about. But—take it gently. We don't want to stir up a bunch of politicians." It is indeed a strange and wondrous thing that politicians, who swear allegiance to law and order, scream very loudly for copperly blood, given half a chance.

"Right, sir," said Inspector Cruse.

"Keep it under your hat," the Chief commanded. "Don't spread it about."

Councillor Mrs. Bagster was preparing to go out when the phone rang, and the friendly young voice at the other end identified itself as belonging to a policeman, requesting an interview. She made the round of her shops usually on Saturday, just to see how business was doing on this, the peak day of the week. Stalwart knees immediately trembling, receiver quaking against her ear, she said:

"Ah, yes. Yes. When?"

"Right away, madam, if it's convenient," the policeman said. "I can be there in ten minutes."

"Yes. Yes. All right." Shaking all over, she put the instrument down and made way to the whisky bottle. Alone in her big, beautiful house—her husband was on the golf course, as ever—she waited.

The policeman, when he arrived, was indeed young; and tall, broad-shouldered, very pleasant in manner. Handsome, really, in a decent suit. So much for riches. Her husband wore much better, but looked much worse. The young policeman smiled, white-toothed, at her when she answered his ring of the bell. "Good morning, madam. Inspector Cruse." He flashed his identity card.

"Ah, yes," she said. "Come in."

She stood aside, so that he could enter. A good policeman uses more than his eyes. He smelled the whisky on her breath as he passed and waited politely on her thick carpet while she closed the door; he saw the glistening of her face. But he said with all his charm as she led him to the drawing room: "Lovely day, isn't it?"

"Yes. Lovely." And it was, radiant with the new-come heatwave, July sunshine not yet drowsy as it would be in the afternoon.

"Nice room." The young man—absurdly young, as many policemen are to people over forty—glanced around appreciatively as he came into it. "They knew how to build in those days, didn't they?"

"Yes. Yes, they did."

"Well—I mustn't presume upon your time." Very polite. Spoke fair English, too. A trifle pedantic, perhaps; but what would you, in a copper getting down to nitty-gritty? "Just a few questions, if I may. About your unfortunate affair."

"Affair?" The word has different connotations. The councillor swallowed. It makes observable movement in the throat.

"Your break-in."

"Ah, yes. Yes."

"No solid progress this far, I'm sorry to say, but we're working hard on it." There—that was softly-softly enough. A plug for us and a touch of soap, all at once. "We were wondering as a matter of fact, whether there was something else in the soap."

"In the soap?" she said.

"Did I say soap? I beg your pardon—something I was thinking about. Safe."

"The safe?" she said.

"Mm." Bland, the attractive smile, and the blue eyes clear and guileless. "Something somebody may have wanted. We think the theft of the money may have been a blind."

"Nothing was in there. Only the money. And the books."

"Uh-hnn. Can you think of anything, anywhere on the premises, that might have been the real objective?"

"No." A bright smile twitched suddenly over the lady's square-jawed glistening whiteness. "What sort of thing?"

"Ah. Now that, of course, we don't know. We thought perhaps you would. Have you ever heard of a man called Frank Daly?"

Literally, she swayed, skin pallor toning to gray. Christ, he thought—she's going to fall down; but she sat instead, suddenly, in a beautiful leather armchair. Sitting splay-legged so that her great stockinged thighs showed, and a portion of what looked like directoire knickers, she said:

"You—excuse me—I have—these dizzy spells—sometimes. These—dizzy spells."

"Can I get you anything? A glass of water?" Aspirin—Digitalis—slug of Vat 69, something like that? Though a slug or two you've had already.

"No—thank you. I'm—quite all right." The big plastic beam twitched out again, all those teeth too evenly matched like a string of domino-shaped cultured pearls made by an oyster who hadn't quite got the hang of it, and too white against the grayed skin. "I—have to go out—soon."

"Yes—yes, of course. If you are sure you're all right, perhaps we can—well—press on, so that I can get out from under your feet." The policeman's smile was much the more attractive. People normally liked Inspector Alec Cruse's smile; they said it warmed them. People who were not Councillor Mrs. Bagster, this sunny morning.

"Yes," she said. "Yes."

"Now—where were we? Oh, yes—Frank Daly. He's a—well—a criminal. A gangster, really. Or he was, in Ireland before he came here." Qualify; because we've never yet managed to pin the bugger, and it doesn't do to paint a man too scarlet when conversing with a politician serving the constituency in which he lives. Especially when that politician goes gray at the mention of his name.

Now why would she do that? Graft? Backhanded monies accruing? But what could she do for the like of Mad Frankie? And anyway, she had a lot of money.

"Ah," she had said; and was sitting looking up at him, still with the beam in glistening place. Yeeurck—those knotted thighs and plastic choppers. Time to speak again.

"We have reason to suspect that he may have been behind the

break-in. It really doesn't add up, that he'd bother to rob a shop or have it robbed for the sake of £400, and two hundred of those traceable notes. That's why we thought perhaps there was something else—maybe not in the safe at all."

"No," said the lady in the directoire knickers. "No—I told your Sergeant Rosher—only the money. That's all they took."

"Yes. Yes—it's in his report, of course. Well, that appears to clarify the situation." Does it buggery, we're exactly where we started. Except that you have gone oddly gray. Very peculiar color. I smile upon you again. "Thank you very much, Councillor, for sparing us so much of your time."

"Is that—all?" she asked.

"Yes. Yes—most helpful. Thank you." Tall and ruggedly almost handsome the inspector stood, obviously waiting to be shown out; and thinking: Let's see what happens when she tries to get up.

Nothing much. She arose, and the hand that gripped the chair arm to steady her could have been there to cope with one of those normal seconds of imbalance, or indeed the lingering aftermath of a dizzy spell. Women tend to dizzy spells at a certain age, and hot flushes. But unless she had gray blood, she wasn't having a hot flush. Steadily enough she led him out from the lovely room, across the elegantly proportioned, antique furnished, and richly carpeted hall, and he smelled again the whisky wafting about the plastic choppers as she opened the door to get rid of him.

Almost before he was closed into the car and had driven away down an immaculately graveled drive between barbered lawns and neat flowerbeds, she was on the telephone to Frankie, not long up and engaged with a bowl of Rice Krispies. Into his ear, without a word of identification she erupted hysterically.

"Did you rob my shop? You robbed my shop!"

"Who's that?" he said. "What shop?" The Krispies snapped, crackled, and popped in the bowl.

"My shop," she cried. "Why did you rob my shop?"

"Don't be a silly old bag," he said, the wicked laughter rising up in him. Because he knew who she was, all right. And although his choosing her for victim was intended as a private jest shared only with Jokey, he didn't mind at all that she had tumbled. It thickened the rich cream. Not a thing she could do, while he had those photographs, without bringing upon herself utter disaster. "I don't go around robbing shops."

"Liar!" she gabbled. "You're a bloody liar!"

So he snapped at her. Not really annoyed, but it was first thing in the morning, for him. Dammit, he was still in his dressing gown, and the pop departs from Rice Krispies as soon as aural attention is diverted, and they go soggy. "All right, all right—so I'm a bloody liar. Just don't tell the insurance company your friend did it, and where's the harm done?"

"Friend?" she cried. Almost, she sobbed it. "Friend?"

"What else am I? But for me, you'd go to jail." He was smiling again before the phone clacked into its cradle. Not a bad exit line, that. She wouldn't, of course—she wouldn't go to jail, in spite of the childlike look of her two co-frolickers. Lesbian ladies are not jailed nowadays, however kinky their manifestations; but it was a nice line, no less. He must remember to tell Jokey when he arrived, if only to needle him. The way Jokey scowled and muttered about farting around was a constantly recurring small sip of cream. Useful little men, the Jokey Fentons of the world; but lacking imagination, and so without sense of humor. That's what kept them from rising to the heights.

When Sergeant Rosher came in for lunch he went up to the bathroom to make a little water, as people often do. Much relieved, he emerged onto the landing, just as the young girl came out of her room, stark naked. She held a towel loosely in one hand, where it did nothing at all in the cause of concealment; until after the initial moment when both were stilled, she moved it, to cover half-grown, pink-tipped breasts and the new neat blonde tuft. If anything, the effect was more devastating than complete nakedness. Delicate shoulders bare, curved body bare behind and beyond the edges of the towel, slim legs bare, she said:

"Oh—sorry. I was just going to have a bath."

"Ah," said Rosher. "Hrrrmph. Ah." He went on down the stairs. The child moved on, into the bathroom.

It disturbed him. When a man, for reasons to do with a fat wife, has carried a libido more than usually rampant through the better part of his life, it may lie quiescent for a while under the combined effects of mental shock and depression and inadequate diet, especially when the castration problem stemmed from the libido itself; but it never dies. Feed the man—ease the depression—and here we are again. So the Sergeant, fed and eased, felt as he went on his way to where the soup was already being ladled into his dish, the old under-trouser stirring.

What disturbed him, in truth, was not the sudden urge to lechery with a girl not more than thirteen years old. Only the sentimental soul colored still with Victorian primness believes children to be sexless, and a man damned forever who responds to puberty's new loveliness. The police, from long acquaintance with incest and the doings of aging men in cinemas and church halls, know the thing that psychologists and teachers know: Humanity is born randy. Rosher's tastes had never been directed to little girls; they were fixed on biggish women, well bummed and breasted. It was one of these that brought him low; and what disturbed him was the mere fact of interest in *anything* feminine, stirring in the jungle between his thighs. He was through with all that; but it appeared the appendage wasn't.

He said nothing about the happening to Margaret, who served him as quietly and competently as ever; but his eye had retained the image of that beautiful body; and now he saw—ah, but his deeper-level mind must have seen before this?—the breasts on this woman, the roundness of hip, swelling of buttock and thigh. And clear through the glorious perfume of steak and kidney pudding—even on hot days he retained contempt for salads and the like—his alerted nostrils found her scent. He left the house with his erectile tissue doing the job it had failed in these many months past.

It was the child who spoke of the happening to Margaret. Clean and shining as a new pin, she came down the stairs when

Rosher was gone and said: "Where is the old bugger?" Hair in a plait, lips dewy, innocent as the newborn day.

"Back to work," Margaret answered shortly. She did not like either of her children. No affection had arisen with closer acquaintance. "Where were you?" Helen was absenting herself already from the image-building tasks of table-waiting and generally helping Mother.

"Having a bath," the girl said.

"If you got up in the morning you'd be more use about the place." Experience in brothel control brings the ability to measure snap into the voice without provoking riot.

"That's a treat, isn't it, get up and work?" The girl didn't speak badly. Fair accent, passing easily for southern. Matched reasonably with Margaret's own stage-school-fostered clarity; only the vowels went to pieces when she relaxed or lost her temper. The boy was the one who had to keep his Bradford mouth shut; but then, he was seldom in; and since Rosher scarcely heard either one say more than good morning and good evening, differences in accent had never registered in his ear.

"Some of us have to do it." Margaret was washing up by now, bringing the crockery glistening wet and white out of the white Squirtie suds. The new milder-than-mild Squirtie. Fifty coupons and you get a garden gnome.

"That's your job, isn't it? Mine's to get him up to the old how's-yer-father."

"No, it's not," Margaret answered, sharply. But she knew the born whore. What was the good? "Your job's just to be here. That's all. You don't have to do a thing. Except help me."

"He's going to be fixed for shagging me, isn't he?" The barrack-room word tripped lightly out from virginal lips. Pretty, pretty thing, with her pearly teeth, her wide, clear eyes, and her hair tied all in a plait.

"That's not necessary." Margaret did not say, as many madams would, he doesn't have to shag you. She never spoke vulgar sexual parlance to her own whores; she wasn't going to do it with this one. Besides, she was under the skin of the part by

90

now. Demure and splendid mothers do not speak that way to wayward daughters. "You're here so that he can be *charged* with offenses. He doesn't have to commit them." None of the family would be here anyway, by the time the charge was pursued. It was all part of the general hoisting of Rosher. They'd be well under cover, leaving a mystery and a laughingstock.

"I just let him have a flash," the girl told her, grinning.

Margaret looked at her sharply. "When?"

"Just now. When he came up for a pee. Walked out starkers. You could see his trousers come up." The grin turning to a girlish giggle.

"You leave him alone," the woman snapped, running her little mop over the vegetable dish. "No sense in unnecessary stirring."

But the young do not listen. "Never had a copper," said Helen. "Had a vicar. Dirty old sod, he was. Never had a copper." She spoke mischievously, almost teasingly, as if she felt dawning in her the urge to remedy the omission.

"You just leave him alone," Margaret warned her. "Frankie won't like it, if you start making complications." At your age, I'd never had anybody.

"Bugger Frankie," the naughty little thing said.

Rosher was back tapping away at his desk before Cruse got to the Chief Constable again, the heat of the day come to that sultriness when men tug at collars and feel sweat attacking in mass formation the scrotum, the small of the back, and the brave, thin line of deodorant under the arms. Drowsiness steals upon the eyeballs willy-nilly and the brain gives off a soporific hum like sleepy bees. It happens to all men; it happened to Rosher, well lined with steak and kidney pudding, plum pie, and cheese. Typing report on his morning activity—no lead left to follow, the job bogged—he found himself nodding as he prodded the Remington with hairy forefingers. Cruse only, among the personnel of the station, stayed fully alert.

Two reasons for this. Firstly, the mental kick it gives to a policeman, when he has reason to suspect that he is on to something. Secondly, he must see the Chief Constable, and a man closeted with his Chief Constable does well not to drop off during the conversation, mouth fallen open and gargling.

The Chief it was who felt a tugging even greater than Rosher's, toward ten minutes of noddies; as well he might, having newly returned from one of those civic lunches based upon chicken, where ratepayers' wine is freely dispensed. Councillor Mrs. Bagster was there; and looking none too well, he thought when he sought her out to offer condolences upon her break-and-enter. Her reply verged on the incoherent, she hardly ate a thing, although she bashed the wine; and every time he looked her way her eyes were just sliding off him. Also, she had a gray face.

Civic lunches do not end smack on the dot of the hour. They start early, and council members drawing solid allowances for the service they are rendering to the community by eating at its expense are in no particular hurry to break things up. So long as the liquor lasts and somebody with a belly made rotund by years and years of it can still stand upon the feet to say something, you will find them there. So it was three o'clock before the Chief Constable came back into his office, popped a peppermint into his mouth, sat down at his desk, and began to nod off. Upon which the intercom buzzed, with savage glee.

The Chief jerked back from a softly encroaching dream of fair women, glupped twice with tongue and lips against the aftertaste of wine and conviviality, pressed the little button, and said: "Yes?"

"Cruse here, sir," said the diabolical instrument. "I wonder if you can spare me a moment."

"Come up." The Chief cut him off, glupped some more, stretched his eyes with his fingers to de-gum them, scratched vigorously the scalp under his thick, tough-looking gray wire, and was himself again.

Inspector Cruse came in, looking alert. "Thought I'd better report as soon as possible, sir," he said. And it's not my fault I've been buzzing at short intervals for bloody hours, while you gluttoned with the town hall mobs. "I saw Mrs. Bagster."

"Good," the Chief said. "She was at the lunch. Looked a bit sick."

"Yes—she would. Something funny there—that's why I thought I'd better see you immediately." Which is as broad as I can hint. Three hours guzzling the rates. And they go up again, this year.

"Funny? In what way, funny?" You would never have thought the iron man was glupping a few minutes ago, and stretching his eyes open with his fingers, and scratching.

"I asked if she knew Frank Daly and she nearly fell down. Went gray—I thought her heart was giving out."

"Indeed? Interesting. Very interesting." The Chief sat back, steepling his fingers in the manner favored by Sherlock Holmes, waiting lion-headed and shaggy-browed for his minion to continue. Silently, he exuded the after-bouquet of a not ignoble white wine. Not a great wine, but relatively impudent.

So Cruse told him all about his conversation with Councillor Mrs. Bagster; about the strong scent of whisky on her so early in the day, and how she went down bump into her chair when he hit her with Mad Frankie's name; and of her denial that anything of value or interest existed in the safe or shop to attract anybody but a person seeking quick money. He dotted each *i* and crossed every *t*, speaking crisply because the Chief liked it that way. When he finished, the Chief said:

"Yes. Very interesting. Not exactly proof of some tie-up between them, of course, but very strong indication."

"May I offer this, sir?" In Cruse was a smug little glow of triumph. He'd done that very neatly, everything in crisp, precise order. Now this.

This was the transcript of the telephone talk between Councillor Mrs. Bagster and Mad Frankie Daly. This is what had made him press his intercom button so often, tishing and tushing when no answer came from the big man's office. This had been waiting for him already, when he got back from Mrs. Bagster's lovely house. This was proof, if proof there ever was.

"Ah," said the Chief Constable, when he had read it through. Then he sat brooding for a moment before he read it again. Then he said: "Well—yes. Calls for another visit to the lady, wouldn't you say?"

"It would seem to, sir."

"Mm. But—not yet. Don't want to upset the cart yet. Keep it on ice, eh? Until the other matter clarifies."

"Right, sir," said Inspector Cruse. Because this was fair enough. Another panic call from the councillor saying that the police had been back with a transcript of their conversation would tell Frankie in words that his phone was under the tap; and no sane criminal goes forward with a big job knowing that the beady eye is already upon him. And Frankie was eminently sane, in spite of his nickname. A man cannot be truly mad and evade for as long as he had the long arm of the law, with a hand on the end of it for twisting into the collar.

7

At the precise moment when Detective Inspector Cruse left the Chief's office, as Detective Sergeant Rosher sat tapping away in the CID room he was hailed by the WPC on duty at the switchboard, who would have been pretty but for girth, feet, and hairy shoulders. Her voice came loud and tinned over the speaker, because desks in the CID room did not have individual intercoms.

"Sergeant Rosher. Inspector Barclay. His office."

She did a good job, this girl, even if the clipped style she had adopted as proper to it made necessary occasionally the poking of a detective's head into her little cubicle, asking what the hell she was talking about.

Rosher had no deciphering problem. Not this time. It was plain enough. Inspector John Barclay, in his office, requested the pleasure of the company of Sergeant Alf Rosher. Transportation of the gorilla body took but a few minutes. And as evidence of Rosher's stirring in the grave, his movement towards resurrection: He left the typewriter uncovered.

"Something for you," said Inspector Barclay. "Ferguson's supermarket. Bradley Road. One of your notes has turned up, they just rang through." He flicked the small official paper across his desk. "Better get over there, huh?"

"Right," the sergeant said. About-face, and he arrived there not long after.

Once, when the breaking of a fiver was a family event, pasting up a list in a store manager's office or beside the cashier's desk produced the odd win. Shopkeepers enjoyed checking for stolen notes, it gave interest to the tedious day, and there was always a chance that you would find yourself, suddenly, asking the customer to wait while you tiptoed off to ring the police, protagonist in high drama at last. But now: small hope. Too busy, the girl who rattles tot-up keys and flings groceries contemptuously down the little chute, and if she tossed into the air at the end of the day all the fivers that pass through her hands, they would flutter to earth like clotted confetti. As for managers: Their heads are filled with problems of stock control, their stomachs are knotted with ulcers, and they toss feverishly all night in their lumpy beds, held back from sleep by gibbering images of the hard-faced men from Head Office who descend upon them periodically at the store to peer and pry and pick at nits; and depart for lunch.

This manager was fairly typical; except that he had been recently promoted, and was so desperate for Head Office approval that when the police list arrived with the standard request for notes to be checked against it, he detailed a clerk to do just that, with all the fives and tens. Alert security resulting in valuable assistance given to the police is the sort of thing that earns commendation from on high. It suggests that in this branch, anyway, shoplifting will be kept to the minimum.

The clerk, a bare-faced boy merely, as anxious to please this new-broom manager as the manager was to gratify Head Office, and bearing already the pasty, sycophantic-smiling, stooped look of the damned, hurried with list and matching note when he found it to the office marked Mr. Hendry (it used to say Mr. Humphrey, but he shot himself), wriggling like a grinning dog in hope of a little happiness. Now, not much more than half an hour later, he stood before an apelike and unsmiling, bandy-legged man. A real-life detective with a black hat.

No real need for him to be standing here, because he did not see the customer, only the note. However, Sergeant Rosher was savoring this new trip out with his uniformed satellite standing by. To make it last, he would interview everybody concerned. So he commended the poor little chap on the sharpness of eye and keenness of intellect that enabled him to match numbers, and said:

"Where would it have come from, to you?"

The clerk hesitated, glancing sideways at his manager as if to speak in his presence freely to policemen was a thing not done. The manager said:

"From the tills. Naturally. All the money from the tills passes through Mr. Upton." The uniform policeman standing impassive in the background had a thought: That could be bloody painful.

"I see." A lot of Rosher's old-time front had come back. In actors the same effect can be seen, when after months or even years of nerve-shattering unemployment, humiliating neglect and self-obliteration by bottle, they are suddenly contracted to play King Lear. Regal they become, all at once. "I take it you keep a check on what comes from which till?"

"Oh, yes," the manager said. "Every penny is accounted for. We keep a very effective control system going. Of my own devising." Let 'em see you are well on top, dribbling the ball and in possession of all your marbles. Because you never know—this might be some diabolical plot set up by those Head Office bastards, to trap him. Bastards. Well, he wasn't going the way of old Humphrey. Whatever they said, there was nothing wrong with his egg layout, or the way he stored his detergents. If there was one thing upon which he *could* pride himself it was egg display. Bastards. But you dare not argue.

"Uh-huh. I'd like a word with the checkout person. Whoever took the money in." A fiver, crisp and new.

The clerk spoke eagerly. "Till six. Gladys Fairbairn."

"Fetch her," the manager commanded; and the little man hurried away. He came back with a girl in the first sweet burgeoning of her English womanhood. Lashes glued on slightly crooked, a chipped front tooth, hair an improbable yellowy white, shoes that gave her two clubfeet and a tendency to pigeon toes. No, she could not remember who had passed the note. As she said defiantly at the pursing of the manager's lips, they was queuing up all bleeding day; she had enough to do without looking at 'em.

The sergeant sent her away. There was no feeling of aggravation in him; it was just as he expected. Nobody looks at anybody, in a supermarket. Even the store detectives, even the hidden eyes scanning closed-circuit television screens are focused entirely on watch for the furtive glance round, the flash of quick hands vanishing a jar of Old Herbert Pickled Onions under the coat. He picked up the note by its extreme edges—no good for fingerprints, of course, paper; but it impresses the onlooker, and Sergeant Rosher was coming back to form—and slipped it into one of the envelopes detectives normally carry in their jacket inside pocket, saying:

"We'll have to take charge of this, sir, I'm afraid. The money will be replaced, of course. I'll give you a receipt."

"Yes. Yes, of course," said the manager; and off, with polite thanks for cooperation and mutual good-days, went Sergeant Rosher and his silent helper, who spoke only when they were in the car, into the radio transmitter; to say that the interview was completed and they were on the way back.

The radio replied in the voice of a tin goldfish. "Message for you. Proceed to Nobs and Nickers, Dinsmore Street. Matching notes received."

"Knobs and knickers?" the policeman said, incredulously. "What is it, a brothel?"

"Don't ask me, mate," the goldfish said. "I'm only reading what's written here." It cut itself off, sharply.

Nobs and Nickers proved more fruitful than the supermarket. It was a small shop, newly opened and as flashily tarted as were the boutiques owned by Mrs. Bagster. Furthermore, the joint proprietors were mincing males, one black and one white and both fully as camp as the manager of her Henshawe Street branch, but older. They called each other darling, and everybody else ducky. Given names they had, of course. Peter Veal (white) and Victor Hedley (black). When they were not calling each other darling they used these, in a way, adapting them to Petra and Vikki. One of them had actually been to bed with Ernest Brownlow, called Bibi; but as he certainly wasn't going to tell the other, who can say which?

Rosher had always disliked the mincing kind of queer. The others didn't bother him—a big, butch inspector in his own station turned out to be one, caught full-handed in the locker room with an equally big, butch constable. He had even felt a certain pity for them both, mixed in with the contempt of the bull-bollicked, insensitive male. At least they'd kept quiet about it, until the super chanced to appear in the locker room when nobody should have been about and there the three of them were, goggling in surprise. The flaunting kind, all tight-trousered buttocks and little tripping steps, wafting in a cloud of perfume, this type he could not stomach. Here were two of them. His hard eye went harder, some of the Old Blubbergut brusqueness was back in his voice as he handled the three five-pound notes and said:

"Any idea who passed them?"

The white one said airily, out of a seamed and sallow face (junkies, are they? the sergeant asked himself; it seemed likely): "No idea, ducky. Lots and lots of people troll in and out, we're very popular. Nowhere like it in town, is there?" Very true, the place was stocked with underpants lettered with the kind of invitation that looks well on urinal walls, cut and molded to accentuate the genitals; with feminine frilly G-strings and suspender belts and bras with twin holes cut in, to let the nubile nipples poke through.

Rosher spoke again, addressing the black one. "How about you?"

Rouge, lipstick, and eye shadow were really the wrong shade, on a black face. But the silk-looking blouse and scarlet corduroy second-skin slacks bulging at the crotch were, presumably, flare to the nostrils of the sexually bent. The bastard's eyeing my copper, Rosher thought as coated lashes batted at the young man who would meet few people like this when he started spraying cars in Coventry. Worth keeping an eye on this place. The black man was speaking.

"How about me what?"

"Do you remember who passed this money?"

"Sure I do, ducky. Served him, didn't I?"

"Can you describe him?"

The white one was looking at the other with the look of the husband who is holding himself in just on the edge of eruption. The black one took on the air of the defiant, head-tossing wife. How old would they be? the sergeant asked himself. Late thirties, the black? Mid-forties, the white? The black one was saying:

"Young. Fair hair. About fourteen, mebbe fifteen. Wore light blue jeans and suede boots with little metal bits at the toes—you know the ones I mean—and a tee shirt with Ohio University on it. Yellow. Blue eyes. Short nose and rather a pretty mouth."

"Would you recognize him, if we can show you a picture?" Rosher asked.

"Yes. Sure."

"What did he buy?"

"One of our peepie bras and a little suspender belt. Like that." A scarlet-nailed hand came up limp on the wrist, to indicate a trifle of black, scarlet-trimmed lace and elastic, one of several fripperies secured to the prettily papered wall.

"Uh-huh." Rosher noted it all down. Unless the lad wore them himself—surprising how many do, in company or for solitary sessions of masturbation—he had a girl friend. Or something. You couldn't rely on it, these days. Not much of a lead, but better than nothing. Looking out photographs, bringing them here and back to the supermarket—it was all time away from the office. So quite cheerfully he made his notes, issued a receipt for the money, placed it in another of his envelopes, and left, treading too heavy with his heavy-footed companion through a setting designed for tripping. He would, he said, be back. As they neared the door they heard the white one say:

"Never miss a young one, do you? Rather a pretty mouth—it's all you can think about, you whore, isn't it?"

"Oh, for Christ's sake, darling," the black one said. Wearily, it sounded as though the quarrel started long ago, before this specific boy entered into it. "Jealousy will get you nowhere."

"They're a couple of right ones," the constable said as he let in the clutch.

"Mm," said Sergeant Rosher, and settled back in his seat with a very fair description of his housekeeper's son written into his notebook.

If the police's right hand had permitted the left one to see what it was doing, a good deal of time (and this equates to rate-payers' money) and aggravation could have been saved, right here. Because while Rosher was sorting out from the files mug shots of all the juvenile villains in the parish—but not really all; some of the best were too young as yet to have graduated from protected juvenile delinquency into the man's world of finger-print and photo and list of previous convictions to which they would surely come, following in Father's footsteps—upstairs, in the Chief Constable's office, that formidable man was studying a blowup of the very lad he wanted in the very outfit described, coming out of Rosher's own house. While he looked, he listened—to Inspector Alec Cruse, who read aloud from the official form, and had been doing so for some time.

"... breaking and entering, Bradford, October '75. Remand school—borstal—breaking and entering, Bradford, April '76— no more after that."

"Getting better at it, presumably," the Chief Constable remarked. "Not a bad looking kid, is he? The sort you wouldn't mind having as a son. Just goes to show. And nothing known on the women, you say?"

"Nothing as yet, sir. Something may come later."

But it wouldn't. Agreed, the photographs taken from the barn had not been long out, circulated by teleprinter. Bradford had responded at once, because one glance led the feet straight to Jimmy's file; but the other child had not as yet been copped, and the only charge against Margaret was for soliciting, when Nobby paid her fine and ended up married to her, five years ago in Hull. A woman can change considerably in five years, especially when any photograph taken then, before she came to eat well of her own excellent cookery, must show the thin starveling look of a hungry repertory actress.

The Chief was brooding over the Jimmy shot. "Jimmy Burt," he mused. "Now what the hell is going on? And who's the older woman? His mother?"

"I don't know, sir," Cruse said. No way he could know, really. Jimmy's father (deceased), was bent as an old flue brush, but there was no file on his mother, poor lady. He'd have known all about her if the lad had been his parishioner; but she lived in Bradford, struggling for a respectability that had never been hers, and never would be as long as she had Jimmy for only son.

"Mm. Curiouser and curiouser. Well, keep a tail on Rosher, and put one on the lad. Nothing more we can do about it, at this stage."

"Do you want me to rake Eddie Greenwood in?" Cruse asked.

"Eddie Greenwood?"

"The bloke with the telly set. If that's Bertie Smithers with him, it has to be bent. No marking on the van—suggests the set's hot."

"Oh. No. No, let it lie. I don't want anything rocking the boat."

This was the night when Rosher's lurking libido moved out again, encouraged by food, domestic order, basic loneliness, and the good feel of working again in his own natural element, into the open. Not in the old rambunctious way, snuffling for tits and bums with the ravenous hunger engendered by revulsion from the fat ugliness of his wife's accouterments and despair at his

102

own aging. Rather, it crept up on him, on a sudden wave of tenderness.

Inevitable, of course, that it should come back. He had in his house a very attractive woman; and a woman not one's own, domestically engaged in pinafores and indoor frocks, stands in intimate relationship to a lone man, she is half naked already.

He also had in his house these two children, and of what they were getting up to, he knew nothing. For instance: He came home for dinner and went out again, on another tour of the places where criminals take in liquor. Not really to do with the case he was working on; but something of his interest was returning, and it seemed a fair idea—who knew, he might be out and about again, from here on—to reestablish old contacts. A detective has no power, and no chance at all without his contacts.

So he left the house about seven o'clock, telling Margaret not to wait up, just leave a sandwich. By ten past, Jimmy was in young Helen's room with a fancily wrapped package hidden behind his back, saying:

"Get your clothes off and I'll give you something."

She looked up at him, from the bed where she was lying fully dressed, reading a picture magazine designed for semi-literate young ladies (they have to be able to read the captions) who dream of nestling in the arms of curly haired, square-jawed lads six inches taller than they, after trial and tribulation. "I bet you will," she said.

"No, I don't mean that. I got a present for you." He let her see the package.

"What is it?"

"Get your gear off and I'll show you."

Nothing loath. That was Helen. She'd have stripped anyway, because she took pleasure in it and knew she was about to as soon as he came in. It was sooner than expected, that's all. Any woman teased with a present has to know as soon as possible what it is. In under the minute he had fastened on her the black and scarlet peepie bra with the holes in it—not yet could she do

103

it full justice, but she tried her best—and girded the new fluffy triangle with the matching bit of elastic and lace that the trade called, for want of a better word, suspender belt. Two minutes later he was proving that the designer knew what he was at, when from his own lascivious brooding he doodled them on to the paper.

Margaret knew what was going forward. Not about a gift designed to embellish, she had no idea of what this fool of a lad had done; which was to take some of the new money and add it to his own share of the boutique proceeds. Admittedly, he did not fully appreciate that all the notes were numbered; but he should have done, his antecedents were good. Admitted again, the father who might have kept him from such foolishness died when he was young, but he'd known plenty of people since. Greed, is what did it. Pure greed. And he used the notes to buy the fripperies.

But she knew very well what the relationship had come to, and her nerves were not soothed by the knowledge. The truth is, even without this juvenile complication, she was regretting the situation she had given herself to. Basically, she was not at all an adventurous woman. Marrying Nobby—and he was not attracted by sense of adventure; as an adventurer himself he loved a quiet woman—had given her life the twist that led to five years as madam of a brothel. She went into this, when Frankie offered, numb with grief and shock; and because she was by nature not the actress she had believed herself to be in her early days but a purely domestic woman, her house was scrupulously run, elegantly furnished, pin-clean, and a pleasure to work in. All the girls said so. Which meant she had no trouble from them and very, very little from her clients.

But she did not really settle to the life. It simply did not matter particularly what she did, lost in a world without Nobby. This at least fulfilled some of her domestic vocation: She had the girls almost for children and the house to run, and she could cook whenever she wanted, for all of them, giving the lady who normally did it time off. It wasn't like doing it for Nobby; but what

104

was the alternative? A regular job—and she trained for nothing but the stage—a small flat, and a lone chop under the gas grill? Because she wanted no other man. Well, not often; and when she had one it was for body need only. Nobby would understand.

Well, five years of brothel living leaves few illusions about people and sex. In hatred nurtured over those years for the author of all her grief she jumped when Frankie proposed vengeance; and as soon as she saw the two children he had lumbered upon her, misgiving set in. But hatred drove her on; until it was too late to back out. And the heck of it was that even her hatred had less edge to it, suddenly, because here was a domestic situation that needed righting, if ever one did, and a sad, aging man where she had built a monster. Fulfillment of vocation brings irresistible softening to the mind; and a woman finds it difficult to hate a sad man as viciously as she would wish.

Which is not to say that she underwent loving conversion; but she hated now less blindly, and she saw the absurd danger she and Frankie between them had run her into—exaggerated by the actions of these two little bangers. This evening they were in bed less than a quarter of an hour after he left the house. She knew it, she heard the randy little horror go into the girl's room, as he seemed to do all the time now. At fifteen, the thing is insatiable. So she went up and opened the door.

There they were, at it. The girl, legs folded around his plunging body, seemed to be wearing a scarlet and black scrap of lace about her waist, and a matching bra. No surprise—Margaret had seen 'em dressed in anything from Victorian corsets through schoolgirl bloomers and gymslip to the diver's suit favored by a parish clerk who liked to be trampled on by the big lead-soled boots. So she snapped:

"Couldn't you wait?"

Neither made answer. It is not to be wondered at. She waited herself, until the plunging and gasping were done. Then she said again:

"Couldn't you wait?"

The girl looked across from her straddled position. Eyes wide and limpid as always, and completely unabashed. She was, of course, used to having an audience. "What for?"

"He's hardly out of the house, is he?"

"So what?" the boy said. At fifteen, it doesn't even tire one. They really were a pretty sight, cleanly young bodies not yet wrecked by booze or a diet of cream puffs, or whatever method they finally chose for their degrading. The lad was into drugs already, but so far in a very minor way.

Margaret was too used to pretty young bodies even to glance at them. "Suppose he'd forgotten something?" she said. "Suppose he came back."

"Well, he didn't, did he?" said Jimmy. And Margaret's mind was saying:

Wouldn't really make any difference if he did, would it? He's never been near these rooms since he handed them over, except to pass the doors on his way to bed and down in the morning. But even so. . . . She snapped:

"That's not the point. We're here to do a job, not to enjoy ourselves."

"Oh, for Chrissake," said the boy, and began gently to ease his small buttocks up and down again; while the girl, unheeding, said for needling mischief's sake:"

"We've done it while he's been in. Haven't we?"

The boy grunted.

"Do you know you can hear it right downstairs?" Not true; but she had heard the unmistakable sounds from the landing, as she came up. And, dammit, the man was a policeman.

Now the girl rose onto one elbow, impatiently pushing aside the boy's moving hands. She spoke to Margaret. "Oh, bugger off. I'll do what I bloody well like."

The generation clash is not a matter only between children and parents. Margaret snapped again, "Will you, indeed? Oh, will you? You'll do what I tell you."

"Yeah? Get her." Latent viciousness was showing now

through child mischief in the clear eyes. "I'll tell you what I'm going to do, Mum. I'm going to make him. Tonight. When he comes in I'm coming down; like this. Looking for my teddy bear, didn't know he was there. What'll you bet I don't make him? Eh? What'll you bet?"

"You stupid little cow," Margaret said, and slammed the door, leaving them to it. Seething, she went downstairs.

Better ring Frankie, she told herself. Because the vicious little bag would do it; she could mean it. And whether she makes him or not—she very well might, you never know how an aging man will react—when she starts to perform he'll know at once he hasn't got hold of any shy little virgin. Once he realizes one of us is a tramp, he's going to start looking at all of us, a steak and kidney pudding won't hold him.

Yes, ring Frankie. It's probable that she's only threatening, to rile me. But you know what they're like, these kids who think they rule the earth with what's between their legs. Unpredictable. You never know what they'll do, once an idea sprouts in their tiny little minds.

She went to the phone reluctantly. Nobody likes to admit they can't cope, and never before had she needed to call upon Frankie's assistance. Except, of course, when the Neal Road gang tried to take over his business. But then, she'd never been in this situation. A quiet word from him might bring home to the girl what could happen to that pretty face if she didn't do exactly as instructed, and no more. She dialed; and, of course, Frankie was out. Where would a well-heeled and handsome Irishman be on a Saturday night but in or en route for—it was still only seven-thirty—a restaurant somewhere, with a nightclub to follow? Living it up, with a pasty-faced little man watchful at his table, well-honed knife in the sock.

All right, she said, I'll handle it myself. But softly. Don't go up and force an issue; the little bitch will certainly act up if you do, just to show you can't muck her about. And he'll join in—he's as vicious as she is, and as unstable. Leave them to get on with it—just stay on guard, to deflect her if she tries anything. She wouldn't come naked—she'd have a nightie on, at least. Get in first—the maternal reprimand. "What are you looking for, anyway, darling?" Even she couldn't say him. She'd have to say teddy bear. Well, probably not teddy bear, at her age; but handbag, or something. Accidental blundering in. It might prime him, but it wouldn't dent the image. And I'll get on to Frankie in the morning.

This, then, is how it came about that Rosher, when he arrived home, found himself hooked by the libido, on a sudden wave of tenderness.

He was in fair form after an evening spent among his onetime whispering men. Many got away when they saw him coming, but some were cornered, and a few stayed on with covert sniggers playing just under the surface of their chops, hoping to extract a rise from him by such means as slight emphasis on sergeant and its constant repetition when they addressed him, so gathering some small, sweet recompense for all the years of humiliation suffered under his ill-concealed contempt. He soon disabused them. Much of the boomph was back in him, and for some reason he had as yet not analyzed—he wasn't an analytical man—the mental muscles seemed to be growing stronger all the time.

So he came out of his car onto his drive humming horribly, being without a note of music in his makeup, and trod toward his front door in perfect ignorance of the car that went straight on when he turned into his street, one trilby-hatted passenger in it speaking into a microphone that homed his voice into the ear of a man in the barn opposite.

Into his house he came still humming, pleased anew with clean-smelling order; crossed the hall, pushed open the door to his living room—and there she was in pajamas and dressing gown, fast asleep on his settee in front of the still-talking television, soft in the soft light of the lamp used to ward off eye strain. Black and white is trying, viewed in the dark.

A sleeping woman is a potent thing, especially if she does not snore; and Margaret was not snoring. She wore pajamas and dressing gown to emphasize the fact that in her family they all went to bed at a respectable hour, and to establish by this declaration that other fact implicit therein: If the child appeared half naked, she had just got out of bed after hours in it—which, in fact, she had spent, but doubled up—and when she heard the key rattle in the front door lock, followed by Rosher's strange humming, she fell asleep at once, fighting fire with fire in a very becoming posture.

The first thing he noticed was the unexpectedly talking television just coming to where all would fade into a little dot, and the glow of lamp light over the room; and her sweet perfume. The next thing he focused upon was herself; and immediately, in the unguarded second before the conscious mind has time to adjust its shield, he was swept by the wave of tenderness.

She had tied her hair back in a ribbon, and the fact that it was a wig (she brought three with her, as some sort of disguise just in case descriptions were bandied about) made no difference, since he didn't know it. Her dressing gown was blue, pure as the gowns of saints in heaven and as clean, with the legs of sprig-patterned cottony pajamas and neat, bobble-slippered female feet showing at the bottom. She half lay on his settee—body a graceful curve, head against the fattest of his fat wife's hand-wrought fat cushions, rested on a slim, fine-fingered hand. The other hand lay in her lap and her long-lashed eyes were softly closed, one ringed still very faintly with the mark of the brute. On one sweetly curved cheek, too, the marks still showed; but she was making them fainter and fainter, the problem being to get them each time in the same place. Softly she lay there, breathing evenly and with only the childlike sound of it, and her unadorned bedtime lips were curved and innocent, like a child's.

He saw her as a child, in that unguarded second. A child's innocence, a child's fragility—but she wasn't really a fragile girl, she carried a certain plumpness, as good cooks often do—a child's touching vulnerability. He who had never liked children saw her as a child, and was swept with tenderness.

There he stood looking with hairy nostrils snuffing her perfume, for so long that she thought: I'd better open my eyes; if she comes down I want to see her quick, get the first word in. She sighed and let her lashes flutter, and through them she could see now a thing nobody else in the world had seen: soft light in the little hard eyes, a strange remolding of the thick lips and fighter's jaw. She let her eyes open all the way; gave it a second to register; saw him standing there; sat up in bemused alarm, hand flying prettily to her mouth as she said:

"Oh!"

"Don't worry," he said. "Don't be scared—it's only me."

"Oh—I—I—must have fallen asleep." A hand fluttered, to push in the age-old feminine gesture at a tendril of escaping wig.

"Yes," he said. "Yes." Out came his great white handkerchief and he blasted silence; coughed as he tucked the sheet away. She held her maidenly awakening without visibly jumping, nerve-galvanized by his sudden trumpet; said when the air had pieced itself together:

"You gave permission—our set doesn't seem to be—I think they put it in wrong—" Wide open now, her eyes, expressing confusion at being discovered onstage, sleeping.

"Yes, yes," he said. "Quite all right. Delighted. Of course."

"I wanted to see the play," she said. "I thought you wouldn't mind—"

"Not at all. Anytime."

"I must have fallen asleep."

"Ah. Mm. Yes—seems like it. Well, no harm done." And now she was a woman, all soft curves and scented skin, vulnerable as she had been in his seeing her as child. More so perhaps, because of the tiny trace of what would be wrinkles, forming at the corner of her hurt eye.

"I've—your sandwiches—they're here—" She indicated the covered tray, still confused and embarrassed; and thinking: Is that her now, on the stairs? Listening at the door, is she? Or is the other little sod still riding? But I think he went out.

110

"Ah, lovely. Thank you." The big, beige teeth bared themselves suddenly, almost shyly; like a boy's smile when he fears rebuff.

She had risen to upright on his settee. Now she stood. Mustn't leave him yet. "Would you like a cup of tea?" she asked. "I can soon put the kettle on."

"That would be nice." He'd have made one, anyway. He liked a cup of tea when he came in, even with a pint or two of beer inside him. And a pint or two is all he ever drank. Very moderate drinker always, especially when duty had him out among the liquor. A teetering copper misses things.

"I'll get it."

"Thank you." The tentative smile settled more securely. "Nothing like a cupper."

She went into his kitchen and stood on tenterhooks over the high-speed kettle, willing it to whistle (it did this, from a gadget on the spout) and too preoccupied with listening for sounds telling of the child's arrival—voices; expostulation, perhaps—to concentrate on hating him. As the kettle gathered itself to shriek, after what seemed a long, long time, she whipped off the gadget and wet the waiting tea leaves. Then she gathered what was needed while the solution brewed, to near black as he liked it, checked the wig to make sure it hadn't slipped, and went back into the living room, carrying pot, milk, sugar, cup, and saucer on a tray. And a strainer. She brought the strainer. No domestic woman, however preoccupied, can tolerate tea leaves wodged at the bottom of the cup.

All was quiet. He had switched off the television, but left the room soft lit only by the little lamp. A coffee table had been moved across to the settee for the tray to rest on, and he sat now against the lesser fat cushion, at the far end of the settee from where the matching fatter cushion still bore the dint of her head. She bent to the little table, and his eyes saw the white softness of—bosom. Not tits; there was nothing blatant about it, no smirking self-display. Simply, when everything operated by the law of

111

gravity, her leaning revealed the soft upper swell of clean bosom. As a wife will unthinkingly show herself in the privacy of
her home.

"Didn't you fetch a second cup?" He spoke with awful jocularity. Jocularity never suited him. Now, used to disguise the fact
that he wanted her to stay, it fitted less than usual. "Might as
well have one, now it's here."

She fetched a cup. If she could guard him until he went to
bed, she going up almost at the same time—the little cow
wouldn't seek him out in his bedroom. Would she?

They drank the tea, and they talked. He did, mostly, visited
for the first time ever by the nervous garrulity of the man with a
new-met woman, when he has his mind on attributes other than
her conversation. Because he had no gift for social grace, and
because a quietly receptive woman creates willy-nilly the effect
of being fascinated, he talked some shop. Not current shop—he
said nothing of humiliation, of being downgraded, of his being
chained to a desk. He spoke of times past, of cases unraveled by
Detective Inspector Rosher; and impelled by the feeling of
boomph coming back, he said expansively at last, sitting back
with his jacket undone by now:

"I told you I'm in charge of the Bagster job, didn't I?"

"Yes." She felt her heart jump suddenly.

"Yes. Odd thing, in a way." And he hit firmly the note struck
earlier by young Inspector Cruse. All policemen think alike.
"Why that particular shop? Plenty of others. Why that one?" He
paused, looking at her with raised eyebrows, presenting for her
admiration a detective, thinking.

"Ah," she said.

"Mind you, that may not mean a thing. Not a thing. We have
some idea of the villain. Juvenile, by the description, silly little—feller"—Ooh, he'd nearly said bugger—"passed some of
the notes, all numbered."

"Ah. What does he look like?" I'd take bets.

"Fair. Short nose, blue eyes. I took pictures in, but he can't be
local, they couldn't identify. Wore a tee shirt and jeans. That's

useful, isn't it, these days? Tee shirt and jeans—like saying a soldier was wearing khaki. Could be any youngster. Could be your lad, couldn't it?"

"Mm," she said. It could. Stupid young bastard—it could.

"Well, that's the kind of problem we come up against, in this kind of situation." He sat back, wide open, smiling at her now quite freely, if brownly.

"Ah." Me, too, she thought. Me, too, in this kind of situation. I think I'll get out tomorrow. Sudden death that fool Frankie has lumbered me with.

One other topic brought her some stress. He said, suddenly, after a period when he sat comfortably reflecting upon whatever was filling that gorilla's head:

"I suppose they'll be going back to school soon."

"Who?" she said, thrown by the unexpectedness.

"Why, the kids." Again came the awful jocularity. "I suppose they go to school, don't they?"

"Oh, yes. Yes, of course."

"When are they due back?"

"Back?"

"From the summer holidays." She'll be getting sleepy again, he thought, she's not grasping things very quickly. Well, she'll have had a full day, on the go since breakfast time.

"Oh." She pulled a date out of the air, having no idea as to when children are incarcerated back from the long summer vacation. "Third week in August."

"That's late, they go back before that here. Don't know when, exactly, but I'm sure it's earlier than that. Have to find out, won't we? What do they go to?"

Out of the air now came a name. "Princess Mary's." There was such a school, she passed it often.

"Comprehensive?"

"Er—yes."

"Uh-huh."

To her relief, he dropped the subject; but it touched her nervousness because she had no idea into which scholastic category

Princess Mary's school at Birmingham slotted, or even whether it was coeducational; and schools have registers, easily checked. Oh, yes, she thought, I want out of this.

"Well," said Rosher at last, "better be thinking about bed, I suppose. What's the time? Good God—is it really? Well, well—*tempus fugit,* eh?" The awful jocularity beamed from him.

And so to bed; where she lay awake for some time with her door open, listening for the stealthy creak of the girl's door, the tipping of her toes along to Rosher's room.

But the girl did not stir. She was lying tucked into innocent slumber, girded still with her new finery. Jimmy was out with the kind of friends to whom he gravitated by instinct, losing more money at cards with a tail outside the secret club and someone in the barn to eye him as he came back into the house, and to assess again that he was entering through a back window. As for Sergeant Rosher:

He lay in his bed, and thought: Nice evening. Lovely—she's lovely. Men do marry again, don't they? Have to get a divorce first, of course, but—I think she likes me. . . . And when he finally slept, just before young Jimmy came back through his window, for the first time in many months his dreams were warm, and erotic.

114

8

The next day was Sunday, and nothing much happens on Sundays. Police stations have a fairly busy morning, dealing with drunks who collapsed into their vomit and had to be lodged overnight, and the others carried in fighting who didn't want to be lodged but were. By noon, though, everything is over and things settle into Sunday soporific, weather permitting.

Today it did. Beautifully hot and sunny. Out on the golf course the Chief Constable whacked away, great screaming drives that frightened the hair off anybody in front who did not hear his "Fore." Cruse promised his mother he would not be late for lunch and took himself out for his customary two pints, pausing to watch a model aircraft club as he passed the common land where they stunted their little snarling machines, and wondering whether he should join. Mad Frankie Daly spent a lot of the day in bed, with a hangover and a blonde, and Jokey Fenton honed his knife for want of something better to do. Parsons chumbled sermons throughout the land to congregations of mice and hassocks. Everybody with freedom of choice did it his own way. Rosher worked in his garden, which is a thing he had not done for a long time.

He never was much of a gardener, most of the flowerbed construction and tending was the work of his wife; but orderly inside, orderly outside. Margaret had already dealt with the more riotous growth; so he swapped his black hat for a straw panama, which made him look, said a colleague who once caught him in it, as if he did tricks in a circus for bananas, and sprayed a lot of weed killer around, thus slaughtering where they stood his fat wife's beloved petunias. He also mowed the lawn, watched for a while by two fresh young faces at an upstairs window. They did not offer help, and he had no way of knowing that below the level of the window frame two equally fresh young bodies were finger-pleasuring each other, stimulated by doing it in front of Rosher and amused by the knowledge that Margaret knew what they were up to, when she fetched him out a cup of tea.

At lunchtime the girl was back with her mother on service, wearing jeans and a tee shirt with nothing beneath it. If he noticed the out-peeping of small nipples, he said nothing. A common phenomenon, in these days when bras tend to be jettisoned, especially in hot weather; and with his mind reset against the memory of her nakedness, she was not as yet sufficiently developed to achieve the shattering effect aimed at. He might well have wondered what was going on had he seen the child miming exaggerated lust and lascivious kisses towards him, and the scowling set of the woman's lips; but these things took place behind his back. He ate his roast with all the trimmings, his plum pie with custard, and his cheese and crackers very contentedly, demurely waited upon. When the girl had brought his coffee and finally departed, heading for her room, he stirred sugar in and addressed her mother.

"Busy, this afternoon?"

Preoccupied—there had been no chance to ring Frankie, she was wondering if she could manage it while Rosher took a nap—she replied: "Me?" But did he take a nap? He should do, with all that food inside him.

"Well, all of you. Lovely day. Thought we might take a little run out in the car." The tentative, almost deprecating smile she had seen last night spread across his face again.

"Ah." Not likely. What, a family outing with that little sexpot and the boy with his Bradford twang? You can't get through a whole afternoon without speaking, and they'd probably be fingering each other in the back. "I believe the children are going out. They've—made friends, you know."

"Good," he said. "Very good. They need playmates their own age." And as she thought: The little bastards have got them; he added: "What about you?"

"I've—er—a few things to do—"

"Nonsense." Oh, the awkward, brown-beaming jocularity. "Don't have to shut yourself up in the house all day. Little outing—you've earned it. Don't want you getting all pale and thin, do we? Some lovely country, round here." So people said. In his lifelong opinion, seen one tree you've seen 'em all.

She hesitated. Away would go her chance of ringing Frankie, probably until tomorrow. On the other hand, it might not be a bad idea to get him clear from those two. If Jimmy came out into the garden when the old monkey was there—and he was stupid enough to do it—he'd probably have to talk; and the girl might appear in that scarlet-and-black teaser's outfit, to sunbathe on the lawn. After a moment she said:

"Yes. Yes—all right. I'll have to be back to get their tea—"

He felt in his heart relief bordering on excitement; because, after all, what he was proposing was almost dating, thin end of the wedge to further dates. She must know it, she wasn't a green kid. The hesitation he saw as her moment of decision, whether she would allow him to proceed or cut him off with excuses here and now. Proceed, she had bidden. "They're old enough to get their own tea," he said, beaming wider and more easily now. "We'll have tea out, you and me. Find somewhere in the country. It'll do you good." In his voice a sort of playful warmth that surprised even him. It would certainly have surprised his colleagues, his fat wife, and his little whispering men. "Ready when you are, then."

"I'll just—change. And tell them we're going."

She went up the stairs. The youngsters were in their separate rooms, for once. She told them she would be out until evening, and heard the coldness in her own voice. Changing, she said to herself: Yes, stay out until evening. The way they go at it, they'll probably be in bed together at tea time. But they—even they—should have had enough by evening, surely? It's no good denying—they scare me. I loathe them. And it shows.

She came down in a yellow dress, and Rosher thought she looked lovely. He escorted her out to the car, held the door while she got in—more than he had done in many a year for his wife—and drove her away. From the turning at the end of his road, a very ordinary car fell in behind, at a careful distance; but it left them when he steered from the main highway into the country lanes. Impossible, to tail a car with a car, mile after twisting and verdant mile through dozing villages, over shimmering heath and moorland, through woodlands with July-drowsy foliage heavy all around, and no other traffic about.

Unobserved, then, they walked by a lake, and drove on, and stopped for tea with cream and pineapple chunks at a thatched, chintzy-windowed cottage tearoom run by two widows in a thatched village; and drove on, and called into a thatched pub when the pubs opened, and drove again; and he talked. More, surely, than he ever talked before, to anybody in his life.

Still, he said nothing of all his recent agonies. He told her about his boxer days, linking fights with the various cups and shields and trophies she knew from his sideboard collection. He spoke of his right hook, the weapon that hammered 'em down. Hit with it, they didn't get up. He gave instances.

He ran through more of his old cases. He even dug back to his childhood, which he had almost forgotten until now. He mentioned his father, heavy of fist and hard of eye, his mother equally so. "That's what some of these youngsters need these days," he said. "A few good clips around the ear 'ole." And she, murmuring admiration and quiet agreement as seemed advisable, saw them living together in that tenement house, three gorillas clipping each other round the ear 'ole, this one in short trousers.

Christ, what a bore, she thought. What a crashing, smashing,

118

mind-boggling bore. What makes him think I care who knocked out who in the second, or that his old man died of a ruptured spleen after lifting the front end of a ditched charabanc back onto the road? And not a word about his wife. Which means he fancies me. He'll be bloody lucky.

They drove home by leafy lanes cooling now beneath the setting sun, car windows wound down; under surveillance again from when they came into his road at the end of one of the best days Rosher could remember. When they were in his living room—no sound from upstairs, just plain silence—she said:

"Would you like some supper? There's cold meat and pickles. Or I could cook you something."

It touched him, her offering to cook for him at this time of night. "Cold meat will do for me," he said. "Don't bother to lay the table—" that little minx hadn't done it, had she? That's the young these days, no helping Mother unless they're pushed to it—"I can make do with a tray. Fetch one for yourself, too, of course."

She prepared two trays and made tea. They sat side by side on the settee, he relaxed in shirt-sleeves and slippers, thinking: She likes me, all right. Quiet little thing, makes you want to—well—look after her. Bastard, the husband must be. I'll coax her into telling me all about it, one day. But don't rush her; let her get over it in her own time. Chewing on roast beef tanged up nicely with a pickled onion, he said:

"Good day, that. I enjoyed it."

"Yes. So did I." All I want now is aspirin, to ease the pain you gave me in the neck.

"We must do it again."

"That would be pleasant." Like slap-and-tickle with an orangutan. Believe me, I shan't be here. What I want is out.

Monday, and things moved on in several directions. Nothing showed until the late afternoon, when the first edition of the town evening paper came on sale; by which time, some of the movement had taken place.

Item one: Jimmy Burt had smuggled into the house a quantity of *cannabis* resin, and thus more or less completed the setting up of Rosher. A few things more would, perhaps, be added later, when Frankie finally decided whether to go for credibility, or to send the whole caper into orbit upon peals of mocking, deadly laughter aimed at Rosher and the police both, by stocking the place like a Tangier bazaar; but all the basics were *in situ*.

Item two: Rosher was out and about again with his head full of woman, interviewing the delinquent lads pictured in file photographs; because although the black queer in the shop had failed to identify from them—had, in fact, said categorically that the lad who passed the money was not here—you never really know. Given good reason for unshackling from his desk, Rosher milked it for all it was worth, and was out and about; not knowing that he owed his new freedom to the fact that he was under suspicion and carrying a tail. But for this, the Chief Constable would have reshackled him, by quiet instruction to Inspector Barclay.

Item three: The newspaper came out. And item four: The little whispering man whispered again.

Detective Inspector Cruse took his copy of the paper up to the Chief Constable's office as soon as he had scanned the classified advertisement column. He ringed in red pencil one of the small insertions under the heading Personal; and as he handed the paper to the Chief, folded neatly to show the ringing, he said:

"This appears to be it, sir. Melons."

The Chief Constable read the advertisement keenly. No particular reason why he should display keenness, except that he was the Chief Constable. Nobody tells a Chief Constable that all men know he has difficulty with small print but will not wear reading glasses in public, for the image's sake. "Uh-huh," he said. "Uh-hnn. Unless, of course, the thing is genuine."

"There is that chance, sir, yes." Balls, there's that chance. What, a message reading, "Melanie (Melons). Father fretting, please come home. Mother"? Too great a coincidence, when melons appeared on the code list supplied by the whisperer on

120

the telephone. "If it is Daly, there should be another call soon." The man would ring again, now. This was the arrangement. After the meeting, to supply the final details.

"Uh-huh. What day is melons?"

"Thursday."

A foregone conclusion, really, that melons would be the day chosen for the last briefing before the job. All the days of the week, the whisperer said, had been given an individual code name innocuous in itself, but in slang parlance related to feminine mammary equipment. Bristol appeared on the list, and knockers, and so on. Further evidence of Frankie's Irish humor. No problem, and a merry jest, to work any one of them before the innocent public gaze in a classified advertisement; but melons would be the one used, almost certainly. Thursday meeting, and the job on Friday; when the Securicor van would be holding all the weekly payout money for the three-thousand-odd employees busily fabricating McTavish's Toffees—doubled up this day, because next week the town closed down for what it called The Wakes. Annual holiday, since God knows when.

"Hmm. All right. Any problems?"

"No, sir." Police planning was all done.

"Right. Thank you, Inspector. Any development on the Rosher thing?"

"Only what was in the reports, sir." Account of Rosher's gardening and afternoon outing, so far as this was observable, reached Cruse this morning along with a summary of all the other Sunday movement and happenings around the house, and in what small parts of it could be viewed through the windows, using binoculars from a barn seventy yards away. He brought the typed sheets up here at once.

"Uh-hnn. Wonder what he was doing in the country? Not a country lover, is he? Not a keen hiker, anything like that?"

"Not so far as I know, sir." A man's interests betray themselves in little things. Gardeners tend to earthy fingernails, and if they work in plain clothes they sometimes sport a buttonhole, or they decorate a desk with a carnation in a jar. Country lovers turn up in brogues, they call in on a rest day or are otherwise observed in anoraks and tweedy jackets. Rosher always wore a suit with his black hat, and his boxy shoes were not made for long walking.

"Uh-huh." The Chief Constable's impressive head went down again to his papers, signifying that the interview was over. Once the door closed he would don again the spectacles shoved into his desk whenever a knock came on the door, to see more certainly what he was reading about.

Inspector Cruse went back to his office with nothing to do for the moment apart from all the paperwork connected with other cases. Four days to go before the meeting, the job in five. Too soon, this day, for a policeman schooled in the phlegmatic tradition to feel the onset of adrenaline flow, and for secrecy's sake no other officer would be called in for briefing until the last moment. The Serious Crimes Squad knew already that some of its men would be needed; but it had been told only that a job was pending, details to be supplied later.

At five o'clock the call came through to confirm that it was indeed Frankie's advert. From a public booth, as witness the burping preliminary and the chunk as the twopenny piece fell. Cruse had given his extension phone number and told the voice to speak to nobody else; but it took three minutes for the switchboard girl to push the call through—as a matter of fact she forgot it and left the little man hanging on—so this was his second twopence, and he seemed aggrieved about it. His whispering voice said:

"Take your bloody time, you lot, don't you? Did you see the paper?"

"Yes," Cruse said. "Thursday, is it?"

"Yes. Eight o'clock."

"Where?"

"Harry Fargoe's place. The Happy Wanderer, on the bypass."

Scribbling notes on his pad: "I know it," said Cruse.

"And listen—don't fuck it up. Keep your geezers out of sight, if you got to have 'em there. The one you got tailing me's about as unnoticeable as a fucking great elephant."

"I'll call them all off." Waste of manpower, now. Straight on from here to the finish. Two men, one car could sit in the Happy Wanderer carpark on Thursday evening, just to ensure that the meeting took place. All the details for Friday could come only from this little man, after Frankie's briefing.

"Don't fuck it up, for Christ's sake," the voice said.

"Don't worry, Algy, we won't." But the phone was burring in the inspector's ear.

Terrified out of his mind, Cruse thought; and as he went yet again up the stairs: What a miserable life they lead, the bent. Always a load of fear, never any real peace in them. Except, perhaps, the real fly boys like Frankie Daly. They seem to thrive on it. Wonder if Rosher is one? I'd have said unlikely—but he could have gone sour, after the way the old man's handled him. Tied in with Daly, and now can't get out again, even if he wants to. He knocked once more on the Chief Constable's door; entered when bidden and stood on the carpet just inside, because this would not take long.

"The confirmation call just came, sir. Friday it is."

"Very good, Inspector," said the Chief Constable. "Carry on." And Inspector Cruse went down the stairs again.

Monday, Tuesday, Wednesday. Hot days and warm, scented evenings. Pleasant time for Sergeant Rosher, the evenings particularly so. On Monday he went about again among the clubs. While he was away, Frankie rang his home—from a club where he happened to be, so the call went unrecorded—for a word with the children, as promised. Both were out. He said he'd ring again; and dug the scowling Jokey in the ribs when he put the phone down, laughing to see Rosher entering, wearing his black hat and looking around with his hard little eyes. But neither he nor the policeman acknowledged each other. They'd never even met, except by reputation.

Tuesday Rosher spent at his desk, refreshed by time away, supper last night in company with Margaret (who still felt the need to shield him from the girl) and the growing sense of wellbeing related to these factors; but unable to spin the job out any further. No strong lead to justify it, the case must go into the routine file. What made Tuesday evening so very pleasant was that he took Margaret out. And Wednesday was even better, because he did it again.

Margaret had her reasons for going again into the country with him on those two evenings. Frankie rang on Tuesday morning, and what he said to the kids seemed to have sobered them down; but still she did not trust them; and suddenly, she was visited by quivering unease, perhaps because once unease begins, it feeds upon itself. One fillip, and it can turn to panic.

She spoke with Frankie, of course; briefly before he had his word with the children and at greater length after; when he told her, with laughter bubbling under the brogue, what was planted in Rosher's house.

Well, she'd known about the money and the hot color television set, and she'd had an idea that there would be more planting; but cannabis in already—what if that—or those—young fools decided to sample it, always supposing they had not been on it for years? And if they had, ten to one they wouldn't even try to resist it.

"Frankie," she said, "look—don't overdo it. All I need is them puffing away and stinking the place out—"

"They won't," he promised. "Do you know why? I've told her it's a faceful of acid if she doesn't behave herself, and I've given him a description of what happens to a man's sex life when he's had wire attached to his gear and a generator going. They can have a puff just before you're leaving."

"I don't like it. It's chancy, bringing it all in so soon." I'd thought stuff like this would wait until we were nearly gone.

"Now, now, darling," he said. "Not getting nervous, are we?"

"I just don't see the point in taking chances when they're not called for. He is a copper. Suppose he starts nosing round—"

"It's up to you to keep him looking somewhere else, darling. God gave you the equipment, didn't he?"

There was no point in arguing. If Frankie had decided to do it this way, this was the way he would do it. Suddenly, she saw the whole game clearly for what it was: a highly dangerous prank right from the start, born out of Frankie's vanity—perhaps, even, the need to court danger, to push the luck that comes when a man has been too favored by the gods, for too long. She saw, also, that she had only two courses of action open to her.

She could grab her suitcase and vanish, now, leaving the kids here. But that would certainly set the cat amid the pigeons. Rosher would tear the little buggers to shreds, gifted young villains though they might be. No child, however precocious, can stand up to a tough long-service policeman. And all her treasured bits and pieces at home, mementoes of Nobby, most of them—they'd have to be abandoned. No way back, if she crossed Frankie. She'd have to vanish completely; because once Rosher prized the lid off, it all went back to Frankie—via that bloody councillor, who would undoubtedly spill whatever he had on her and saddle him with a blackmail charge. Oh, Frankie would never forgive; and not only pretty young girls fear acid.

Or she could do what Frankie had suggested and what Rosher's attitude told her would not be difficult: keep him out of the house, and looking the other way.

So when the man came home, he found her cool and neat in a white dress that told of soft woman beneath without needing to screech about it; and he said after his dinner, with a gruffness added to the tentative tone he used on Sunday, plainly in fear of rebuff:

"Lovely evening. Feel like a breath of fresh air?"

"Yes. That would be nice." Quiet-eyed, soft-voiced, comely woman, with her daughter, she said, gone to that youth club. She'd had to say something. God knew where the little tart really was. Or the boy either, for that matter. But Rosher never asked about the boy, who was usually out about his own business, as boys by nature are.

Delighted afresh by her prompt acceptance, he put on the playful air, beaming. "Ah, good. We'll nip into the country

125

again. If you're good, I'll buy you an ice cream." Dominant men, falling in love, address the beloved as if she suffers from arrested development.

They drove by a different route out of town, so that he could display different country; and she endured another evening of his talking. Strange and universal phenomenon, that men normally tight-lipped and taciturn erupt into talking volcanoes under the pressure of mounting excitement engendered by a certain woman.

He talked in the car; during the walk along a high hill ridge offering magnificent views; at the pub where he took her to drink beer, outside at a rough bench as the sun went flaming down; he talked in the car again and at shared supper eaten in his living room. He talked his whole mind and heart out; and she sat and walked and made appropriate murmuring when he seemed to expect it, bored rigid, repelled by him; and in a way, unexpectedly, pitying him, too, this man who destroyed her loving man, this ogre against whom she had nurtured hatred over the years. Woman is born to pity, God help her; and the more swaggering and hard-eyed the crust of a man, the more certain it is that inside lives a mutilated child, weeping for rebirth. A boring child, perhaps, an arrogant and unpleasant child; but a child, nonetheless.

And he felt—cleansed. All his long agony gone, swept away on the flood of his talking; even his lifelong attitudes viewed in a new, interior light, so that he saw and admitted the truth: that most of his life's disasters he brought upon himself. But I wouldn't have done, he said in his mind. I wouldn't have done, perhaps, if I'd had a woman like this. He said good night reluctantly and slept fitfully, waking often to think about her; which bothered him so little he arrived at the station in the morning whistling, to the astonishment of one and all.

He kept to himself still the agony of his final debasement—how could he tell this rare woman of libidinous involvement with another, seen now as cheap and sordid?—but on Wednesday evening, as they sat with the car stopped on yet another hill commanding yet another fine view, he spoke for the first time of his wife. Of the pretty little thing she was when they married, and he a highly regarded young amateur boxer, All-England Police Champion three years running. Of how almost immediately she fattened as if connected up to a foot pump; and he with her until he was being defeated by opponents who would never have touched him with a glove, in the old days. It frightened him back into training, and he subdued the onrush of flesh; but he never regained his ring skills; and she grew fatter and ever fatter, a deep interest in food and cooking increasing to obsession as time went by; until she was repellent to him. He took refuge in his work, and she in food; and so they lived through the years.

"Where is she now?" Margaret asked.

"Home with her mother," he said; and with a flash of new insight: "Poor woman—I suppose it was partly my fault. All that grub—I suppose it was a sort of—compensation. Know what I mean?"

She murmured noncommittally; thinking: she'd need it, too, living with you. She'd need some sort of compensation. They sat for a time in silence, he looking ahead through the windscreen with a sort of frowning sadness on his heavy face. Then he said abruptly:

"We'll be getting a divorce."

"Ah," she said.

He turned his head to look at her; spoke with that terrible, heavy playfulness: "It'll leave me free to marry again. Won't it?" His eyes were filled with meaning, he beamed brownly.

"Yes," she said. "Yes. I suppose it will." Oh, Christ—the fate that is worse than death.

For most of Thursday, the Chief Constable was in company with Detective Inspector Cruse, holding a series of conferences. Briefings, in fact, which under normal circumstances would have taken place here, in this station. But somebody here could be bent, and for sure there was connection between Mad Frankie Daly and Rosher. Telephones leak, and the arrival of strange

127

brass for conclave behind closed doors is a matter of absorbing interest, in any station.

So they drove first to the city, and confirmed with the Chief Constable there that some of his Serious Crimes Squad men would be needed, all other things being equal, in the morning. Armed. Final go-ahead to be given after Frankie's meeting tonight, and the move-in undertaken without further contact, according to this plan. Inspector Cruse then spread a homemade map and they all bent over it, heads nodding and fingers pointing.

It is a fair distance to the city. So on the way back they stopped for lunch at the sort of restaurant chief constables favor; where Cruse enjoyed his smoked salmon, steak with a tossed salad, and strawberry flan with fresh cream, but bothered himself a little over the cheese and biscuits because it would raise eyebrows, all that money for lunch on his subsistence expense sheet. Chief constables do not eat as other men eat.

Also, should he offer the money, or what, for his half of the bill? Or would they be billed separately, by this waiter who looked like a splay-footed and rather depraved bishop?

In the event, he need not have fretted. The Chief Constable settled the bill when it came with notes from a pigskin wallet; and to Cruse's murmur he smiled the rare smile that lit his hard face into sudden unexpected warmth, saying: "On me, lad. This one's on me."

From lunch they visited a sub-station close to home. CID men would be used from here, and from a second such station to be contacted by the Chief Superintendent in charge. This, because to drain the CID of their own station could well alert the sensitive bent, giving time for a furtive phone call even if it took place at the last possible moment.

And now they went back to home; where one by one, single comings and goings being less remarkable than concerted movement, the superintendents of CID and Uniform Branch were seen, and the Chief Inspector who would stay here at the station, in charge of radio communication. Not much for him to do,

128

at least during the early part of the operation. Walkie-talkie and car radio messages can be intercepted too easily by sly listeners fiddling with knobs in other cars; and code is all very well, but it can lead to muddle. Better silence, wherever possible.

When these men had come and gone, long service stalwarts all and wary nonprattlers, the Chief said: "Well, that about sets it up. I'll see to the authorization for arms. The rest is up to you and your phone call."

"What about Sergeant Rosher, sir?" Cruse asked.

"Rosher. Ah, yes. He goes with you, I think. Don't you?"

"Yes, sir." No need to say more. From the second he arrives in the morning, keep him close. All the time, until it's over.

"And if he makes a false move," the Chief said, grimly—but surely not officially? Surely he was joking?—"put a slug into him."

Is he joking, Cruse thought, or just wishful thinking? He's a hard bastard and he doesn't like Rosher. He ought to watch it, saying things like that. I suppose it's a compliment; he must see me as well within the camp or he wouldn't do it, but even so— what if I took him at his word? "Yes, sir," he said.

Inspector Cruse, reflecting upon the condition of the whispering man, hit a nail squarely upon the head. He was frightened out of his wits. His name was Algy Kadowski, an ugly, meager-bodied little troll who lived always in the shadow of fear, as, of course, do all petty criminals, especially those not above grassing, to curry favor with the police or for a trifling handout.

If Algy did not as a rule whisper over telephones or into the ear of a bulky man in a dark place, his forebearance was not based on moral scruple, it had nothing to do with the myth of honor among thieves. There is no honor among thieves. Simply, his fear went deeper, was more a basic characteristic than it is even among the general ruck of the small-time bent. Perhaps the root of it lay in the nightmare flight from Poland undertaken by his parents, humping him on their backs by night and cowering in woods and ditches by day, at the start of the Second World

War. Certainly he had lived with terror ever since; and he had seen what happens to the whispering man, when his friends find out who did it. This is for sure: He would never, never have dared to whisper on anybody so big-time and ruthless as Mad Frankie Daly, who carved up Johnny Heston so that he nearly bled to death and still talked out of a twisted mouth, peered from one nearly blinded eye; but unbalanced hatred can override even fear. Frankie had taken one woman too many.

It goes without saying that Algy was irrevocably bent. Less obvious, unless to the shrewd few who ruminated upon a constantly twitching eye, was the fact that he was, in truth, mentally unbalanced. And he hated Frankie with the kind of obsessive hatred possible only to those tipped or tipping over into madness. If Frankie had realized this, and the ugly little man's general condition, he would never have entrusted to him even the tiny part he was to play in the big job. But then, the original idea came from Algy.

When a man hates as Algy hated, look for a woman in it. In his case it was a young, a very young drab, picked out of the gutter. No woman above gutter-level desperation ever looked at him. He took her off the streets, he fed and clothed her into loveliness. He loved her, idolized her, he who had lived without love of woman all his life, since his mother died almost as soon as she reached England. He thought she loved him. She said she did, she whispered while he caressed her soft places in his bed, she took his hardness in her loving hand and herself guided him into paradise. An unbalanced man's love is as obsessive as his hate.

Then Frankie saw her, the lovely thing Algy had created out of a starveling drab, out of his worshipping love; and took her. For a time. Frankie, handsome, laughing Frankie with the blarney-brogue took many women, and most of them were in love with him. She was. So much so that when he brutally finished with her—his ending of sexual liaison was invariably brutal, it was the only way he could get rid of the stupidly besotted—she committed suicide. In Algy's bed, leaving a note to say why. Until then, he had not known a thing about her affair with Frankie.

130

And Frankie did not even send flowers. Probably he had forgotten which of the mad bitches she was.

Out of this came the hatred that blinded Algy even to his own terrible fear. Ever since, he had brooded obsessively upon revenge, and awaited opportunity.

It knocked when he spotted a newly condemned building in Southgate, main shopping street of the town. On the ground floor a shop, selling up; above, offices moving out; and from every upstairs window an unimpeded view of the bank on the opposite side of the road.

He had worked often for Frankie, in a very minor capacity on small jobs. Now he went to him—in a pool room, the likes of Algy were not encouraged to visit the luxury flat—and pointed to the potential. Every Friday the Securicor van called, to collect all that money for McTavish's payday.

At first, Frankie had seemed amused; but all ideas for big money have some interest to a man who needs to gather it, not only for the spending but for the excitement of doing so by direct and swift action and the need, for his position's sake, to offer his henchmen big tickle. So for once—the best of pool rooms has leaky walls—Algy found himself brought to the flat, where he outlined the idea. Frankie said: "Right in our own backyard? You must be joking, boyo." While Jokey grinned, and honed his knife.

Algy said, groveling doglike, grinning ear to ugly ear: "You could do it, Frankie. You could do it. It's easy—all you need is a bloke up in one of them offices—me, say—with a walkie-talkie. Ain't it? It always comes between nine thirty and eleven, the van. No problem, is it, with him up there to tell you when it's here? I mean—you don't have to hang about in Southgate, do you?"

"And what do you reckon the job's worth?" Frankie asked, still amused. The idea was far from new, walkie-talkie go-aheads are used quite commonly. And he had, of course—who hadn't?—speculated himself, often, upon how much money was in that van when it drove away.

"Well," said Algy, "there's more than three thousand at Mac's, ain't there? And they're all working overtime. It's got to average about seventy, eighty each, ain't it?" He hadn't even been offered a drink. Stood there on that thick carpet, throat bone dry already with heart-hammering tension; and nobody even offered him a drink.

"Not worth it," Frankie told him. "Get some other mug who can afford twenty years."

"Fifteen, with remission," said Jokey; and Frankie laughed.

So Algy left, still without a drink.

But then Frankie thought of Wakes Week, and all those seventies and eighties doubled up with holiday money. More and more, too, the sheer audacity of a big one in his own backyard began to appeal to his Irishness; especially so since he was planning—although nobody knew this, not even Jokey—to quit the backyard very soon. Sick of it, he was. A little more money stashed where he could get at it, and away to lie on a beach in the sun, somewhere with no extradition laws. This could be it— the desirable big tickle, and the kind of spectacular crown to a career that makes of a man a legend in his own well-heeled lifetime.

The longer he thought, the more he liked it; so he put it to Jokey, who demurred at first. But Frankie was not given the blarney for nothing. He knew his man, and what a hint that he was chicken would do, combined with the lure of big money. Jokey won, he rang Algy and said:

"That idea you mentioned. Do you want in on it?"

The invitation was a courtesy, extended as acknowledgment of service rendered. Any one of a dozen little men always ready to run when he whistled could have done Algy's part, which was merely to watch every Friday for several weeks, from a dusty office above the now empty shop, the arrival and departure of the Securicor van, noting time variations and general procedure; and to be there on Friday with a walkie-talkie, two words only to say.

Simple. Anyone of the dozen could have done it.

By the time Thursday came, terror had reestablished itself in

Algy until it ran neck and neck with his unbalanced desire for revenge. He had attended Frankie's preliminary dinner, he had whispered, giving the code and names of personnel present, he had arranged with the police for further calls to be made, when the next coded advertisement appeared and after the meeting to which it would summon him and the other chosen men. He lived out these days in rising panic.

What if Frankie knew—or found out—now, or ever? O Christ—what if he found out?

O Christ!

He'd run. He'd clear out—he'd run.

Where to?

In his fever he gave Frankie wider connections and power than he in fact possessed. Frankie was known everywhere. He'd put a contract out—

And the police—that big bastard tailing him—they wouldn't let him run. The big bastard would have him, before he bought a ticket.

But the police didn't know who was whispering, he hadn't given his name.... And the tail was off.

Or was it? The sods were full of tricks.

Round and round, round and round, the panic in his head. He spent most of Thursday in bed, sweating and even weeping; until it was time to go out, to buy the evening paper; by which time he was in the recurring cycle of thought that said: Do it. Get him sent down—for twenty—the bastard—destroy him—destroy him—the bastard—as he destroyed her—and you.... And above all his terror again—for a little while, a little while—up soared elation, and all the black joy of his coming revenge.

So he bought the paper, to find the advertisement in it, as he knew it had to be after blank Monday, Tuesday, Wednesday, if the job was to gather the Wakes Week money; and he rang the copper.

Now he tied his necktie in the cheap flat to which, unable to bear constant reminder of brief joy, he moved after the girl's death. No way out of the meeting, up at the Happy Wanderer.

Frankie's telephone would have them coming in through the windows with the razors in their hands, if he wasn't there. With quivering hands he jerked at the knot, his ugly little face staring pallid back at him from out of the mirror, the uncontrollable eye twitching like a semaphore under heavy pressure, all the bone glistening under the glistening skin. When the phone shrilled he jumped entirely into the air.

It was Frankie. "Hallo, me buck," he said. "How are you? We shan't be needing you tonight."

"You—what—you—what?" said Algy.

"Shan't be needing you, boyo. You know what to do—nothing else concerns you. Stay sober. Here's to riches." He was gone.

O Christ, screamed Algy's mind: He's tumbled—he knows. With desperate, fumbling fingers he dialed the number he had been given to expedite contact with his copper.

Cruse, working late on arrangements for tomorrow, picked up the telephone in his office and said: "Yes?"

"He rang—he rang," babbled Algy. "He doesn't want me—the meeting—"

"We know, Algy—we know." Frankie rang from his flat. The transcript had just come to hand, whizzed to him as important. Cruse had it in his free hand, was reading it when the phone rang.

"How do you—my name—how do you know—my name?"

"We have our methods, son. And Algy—don't do anything silly, we don't like it. Be there in the morning. All right?"

This time it was Cruse who cut the call short, slamming his phone into the rest and saying to himself: Sod it. Sod it. That turns the bloody applecart over.

The Happy Wanderer, out on the bypass, is a pleasant roadhouse run by a pleasant man. Harry Fargoe, bent as a lavatory pipe. And yet he gets away with it, finger in many a murky pie. Well, some do, and that's a regrettable fact of life. In a room to which this man would admit nobody else until the inmates emerged from their private meeting—he didn't know what it was about, and didn't want to know—sat Mad Frankie Daly, alert and happy as the excitement began to key up within him, running over the details for the benefit of the boys who sat with him.

George (Rummy) Stevens was there, and Eddie Greenwood, he who delivered the color television set to Rosher's house, both of them men of muscle, side by side along the table to Frankie's left. Opposite were Ronald (Fizzer) Sparker with his cauliflower ears and Henry Frederick Thomas, often called Henry Boy. Tough men all, chosen for sheer nerve rather than for any peculiar skills. And at Frankie's right hand sat Jokey Fenton. White-faced, deadly Jokey Fenton, honing his wicked knife.

It was not a long meeting. No reason why it should be, all these men were veterans and the job was straightforward. Neddy Seamon and Bobby Terriss would be driving the cars, they were out selecting them now. The present company needed only to be told who moved to where to deal with whom or what, when those cars drew up and they leaped out with stockings over their heads, dressed in overalls. These matters clarified, Frankie said:

"That's it, then. Me with one gun, Eddie and George in one car; Jokey with you two in the other." He nodded to Fizzer Sparker and Henry Frederick Thomas. "Jokey will have the other gun. Rendezvous ten past nine, corner of the old cemetery road. O.K.? Any questions?"

Nobody had questions. Heads were shaken as his blue eyes moved from face to face, mildly enquiring. Thin spirals of blue smoke arose from cigarettes. Handsome and happy, revelling in his natural element, feeling the tingle in his veins, Frankie said:

"Good. Good. Now we'll have a couple of beers. And no more. Understood? I want you all on your toes in the morning, nobody gets shickered tonight. Tell Harry, will you, Georgie? Pints all round."

They left two pints later, quite openly and in a body. Nothing remarkable about a party of men emerging from a roadhouse, to enter separate cars and drive on their separate ways. They were, in fact, quite unobserved, in the police meaning of the word. All tails had been called off. The longer a tail is on, the greater the chance that somebody will notice. No sense in risking it, at this juncture.

9

When the front door bell rang at seven thirty on Friday morning, Margaret, not long out of bed but neat already, answered it. On the step was a tall, reasonably handsome young man in a decent but not outstanding suit, who smiled pleasantly at her against the background of his plain blue car and said:

"Good morning. Is Mr. Rosher in?"

"Yes." she said. "But I don't know if he can—. He's only just up." Copper, her mind was saying, in a flutter of alarm.

"Will you tell him I'm here? Inspector Cruse." So you're the bird. I'd know you anywhere, from your photo. Not a bad looker, are you? Nicely spoken, too. Wonder where the kids are?

"If you'll wait here a moment—." She left the door ajar; went up the stairs with her heart beating hard. Through the bathroom door came faint scrubbing sounds as Rosher worked up peppermint-flavored foam around teeth that remained definitely beige, in spite of hard labor and the paste manufacturer's hand-on-heart assurances. She tapped. He cried through the bubbles:

"Yeff?"

"There's an Inspector Cruse to see you."

"Oh. Right. I'll be down. Two minutes." Cruse? What the

bloody hell did Cruse want? Another job? Freedom from the desk again? Could be, the tide seemed to have turned. Break-in overnight, perhaps, calling for an early start. "Tell him I'll be right down, will you?" He almost added dear, his mind more occupied with her than with work. A quiet evening at home, yesterday, watching telly with her. She liked him, no doubt about that.

Quietly, she went downstairs. No sound from the kids' rooms. Whether they were one in each or both in one she didn't know, and this was not the time to find out. The copper was still on the doorstep, where she had left him. "He'll be down in a minute," she said; and because she could hardly leave him standing there: "Come in, won't you?"

"Thank you." Cruse smiled his pleasant smile as he stepped into the hall. He showed no surprise at her presence here, made no comment upon it. Instead, when she took him into Rosher's living room he looked around and said: "Rather nice, these old cottages, aren't they?" His automatic opening gambit when he entered a house. It pleased people, the friendly approach relaxed them.

"Yes," she said. "If you will excuse me—." And she took herself away, to the kitchen where the kettle was boiling and the fixings stood ready for Rosher's pre-breakfast cup of tea. Don't stay and talk, don't give him a chance to ask questions. Because even if he knew that his mate had taken a housekeeper—presumably he did, by his attitude—he was bound to be curious. A curious copper asks questions; and she might find herself floundering deep, clutching at answers.

With the door shut, she heard no more than the rumble of voices when Rosher came down. What he said was:

"Ah. Good morning."

Once, he would have called the man by his forename, as likely as not; or addressed him as lad. But that was when Cruse was a constable, and later a sergeant, working under Old Blubbergut. Now that the ranks were reversed, by promotion on the one hand and calamity on the other, deep embarrassment existed between them, so that neither addressed the other by name or even rank, if he could avoid it. Cruse stood in dead man Rosher's shoes.

"Morning," said Cruse. "Sorry to roust you out so early. Job's come up."

"Ah." Rosher felt a further gladdening of a gladdened heart. But he said: "I haven't had breakfast yet. If you'd phoned—"

"Sorry about that—the station rang me, I came straight out. Seemed as easy to collect you on the way." *No telephone call to duty for you this morning, mate. The old man said no phone call, fetch him yourself. Quite rightly. Why take chances? You don't know it, but your phone's fixed. Calls in you can have; calls out you cannot. That way, nobody from here rings Frankie. If the little lady tries it from a booth, the boy in the bushes will have her as soon as she leaves the house.*

Margaret reappeared out of the kitchen, carrying Rosher's cup of tea. "Ah, thank you, my dear," said the sergeant, sudden beam and jovial voice showing more of his feelings than he knew. He glanced at Cruse. "Want one?"

"No, thanks. Hate to rush you, but we'd better get going."

Not altogether usual, but certainly not unknown, for a CID man to be raked suddenly to work by personal visitation from a colleague. Much of the work is sudden. "What's the job?" Rosher asked, and gulped hot tea through the answer. Another thing about CID men: They develop leather guts, from swallowing hot sustenance rapidly, as and where they can.

"Break-and-enter. Watchman coshed, warehouse at Hipwell Green." *Good enough story. People were always getting coshed by night, warehouses were always being burgled at Hipwell Green.*

Rosher turned on again the brown beam, the elephant playfulness. "Seems like I'll be missing breakfast, my dear." *My dear. Small, tentative step on the way to dear—to darling—*

"I'll make you a sandwich," said Margaret, and went neatly, quietly back into the kitchen.

Very soon after, the two men were on their way, in the inspector's car. No real conversation between them once they had agreed that it was a beautiful morning and likely to be very hot later. If the sergeant felt surprise when the car stopped in the town's main shopping area and he found himself following young Cruse to a bare shop commanding a view of all the street opposite and containing assorted ranking brass, he did not let it show. What would have surprised him exceedingly, had he realized it, was the way Cruse was studying his reactions. But Cruse, too, was well versed in the art of not letting very much show.

Groping always in the dark, the police know very well that much of their forward manipulation in any investigation where secrecy is vital must be superfluous. What they do not know is: which part? Ignore a loophole, and that's the one the quarry will dart through. So among other superfluities in the present instant, they fixed Rosher's phone.

There never was any danger that he, or Margaret either, would contact Frankie. It never occurred to her to do so. Vastly relieved that the visit had nothing to do with her or her presence here, she saw the two coppers depart and thought they were off to Hipwell Green. After all, she knew nothing whatever about Frankie's other interest, his big job.

But Frankie did ring her, of course. Just before he left his flat at nine o'clock; by which time, he knew, Rosher would be gone.

The call was brief, and it was recorded; but Cruse did not get a transcript until much later, he being by this time in position and the radio silence clamped down. Frankie said:

"Hallo—Margaret? Turn the girl loose, darling. And then you can all scarper."

Nice feeling for comedy, Frankie. Lit all his fireworks at once, to get the pigs really hopping and give the exclusive inner cognoscenti who would know the full story of the day a real, rollicking belly laugh.

The corner of the old cemetery road is as good a place as any for a meeting of people. It is reasonably inconspicuous, and men

140

climbing into and out of cars, singly or by twos, threes, and fours, are a commonplace; because fronting the road opposite the cemetery entrance is the main factory of McTavish's, who makes among numerous other goodies a world famous toffee. Nearly three thousand imprisoned souls work here in shifts; and many of the lads give their mates a lift, to and from work. No shift finishes at nine o'clock; but night maintenance crews often do, and today's men wore overalls, and a variety of workingman headgear, ranging from battered flat cap to woolen bobble-hat or up-rolled balaclava. And two of them carried tool bags. Long tool bags.

Two cars picked them up, but not together in one cluster. The first, a good but not glittering Jaguar, drew in and took off with the four who stood by the cemetery gates, the man with the tool bag in the seat beside the driver. Half a minute later a Renault 12 appeared and took aboard the group that had just formed, some way along the road. In this car, too, the man with the bag took the front passenger's seat, and both groups boarded amid chaff and laughter, as working men will. The doorman over at the factory, the office staff just arriving in cars of their own, found nothing to wonder at, if they noticed at all. Even gloves don't show, flesh-colored, at a distance. No, it's not a bad place for a pickup. Far better idea than driving all over the town collecting individuals, especially when the men waiting on corners do not even know what type of car to look for. Horns have to be tooted then, or something done to attract attention. Very dodgy.

The chaffing as the men boarded was not entirely stage effect. It continued in both cars as they drove leisurely toward the shopping center. The excitement was in them, the drug that very often does more than desire for easy money to keep the criminal at his trade. They are hooked, on adrenaline. Certainly, Frankie was. Apart from his need for the kick of it there was no reason in the world why he should be doing this at all. That, and the leader's need to impress.

He joined in the overcharged, near-feverish banter; he raised laughs as usual with sallies out of wit stimulated by the excite-

141

ment. No thought of Rosher in his mind now. Behind the quick and easy wit, his mind was checking over the plan.

In the tool bag: the walkie-talkie radio, ready tuned to pick up Algy's two-word message. Heavy metal cutters. And the shotgun. Loaded with blanks, he didn't mean for anybody to be killed.

In the back of the car—shared out by now, among the men who would use them—pickax handles.

In each man's pocket a nylon stocking, or the cut-off section of a tights leg. Stockings are not so readily come by as they were in the good old suspender belt days. All these things duplicated in Jokey's car, the bag held by Jokey himself.

Jokey's car out of sight, cruising half a minute behind, not to be seen now until they came together for the job.

Park in Jover Street, with Jokey waiting in Rose Lane, both these streets leading off from Southgate. Algy would already be in the Southgate office, watching. At his word: move out, both together. The rest: routine.

Make for the guards, the boys with pickax handles. Himself and Jokey, straight to the men with the money, pointing the shotguns. If they resist—fire one, pointed up. It's a rare man will risk the other barrel through his guts at close range. If they're chained to the money, Jokey cuts it away. Any problem—chain won't give or some other snag—bundle the bastards into the cars; all pile in, and away. Cut the men loose and dump 'em.

Separate, and all go home by bus or whatever. The cars on, to be abandoned near London. The money—very hot, and probably new notes, so traceable—away by train with Jokey, all packed in a canvas hold-all. A workman with a hold-all, going to Chester; where a gent named Samuel, who had his own outlets, would pay about half the face value, in old notes, for Jokey to stash before he came back. The hot money would never be seen again, in England.

Simple. He, with this team, had done it before; but in towns far away. Never close to home. It was the very audacity that pleased him, when Algy approached him with the opportunity.

142

The Irish love a venture with audacity in it, and here was McTavish's, right on the doorstep, all that pay doubled up for Wakes Week. Why plan and spend weeks sending out observers? And if the police came sniffing for him—as they would sniff every operator in the country, almost—why, he'd be gone. And all his seasoned lads well alibied. He didn't even need to ask them what they were going to say. What's more, they'd wait with the patience of veterans for the payout. They'd know their share would come when he judged the heat to be off, even if he was no longer with them. Good lads all.

With luck, if the cars were abandoned at Watford, say—close to where they were stolen—the pigs would concentrate on London.

The banter was dying away now, as mounting tension dried throats and took the men beyond the stage of pure exhilaration. The car was approaching Jover Street.

When Margaret received Frankie's command to scarper, she felt a great uprush of relief, almost of surprise. The last few days had been very long and very tense, and she had formed the belief that he would keep her here with these children, perhaps for weeks. Sober consideration could have told her that he would want them out pretty quickly; but sober consideration had sunk under the weight of tension. Last night had moved her mind to something approaching panic.

Rosher had invited her in to watch television with him, and she went; partly because there was no way to refuse, and partly because all day the kids had been hanging around, the girl complaining of boredom and telling graphically what she meant to do with Rosher, the boy, equally bored by now, egging her on. As they sat together watching some damned program mundane even beyond normal, not a word or scene of which penetrated to her strung-up mind, he asked suddenly:

"Any developments with your husband?"

"Developments?" she said.

"Mm. Does he know where you are? He'll have to, I suppose.

There'll be things to arrange and so on. Won't there?"

"Oh. Yes. I—" What was the name of that bloody councillor? "Mrs. Bagster is handling all that—she said she'll get me a solicitor—it's all been a bit—soon."

"Yes. Yes, of course—you need a bit of time. Well, you can stay here, you know that. Long as you like."

"Thank you," she said.

"Will you go back to him, do you think?"

"No. No—I'm—no."

"Uh-huh. Divorce?"

"I expect so."

"Uh-huh." A note of satisfaction in it. The subject dropped.

But it shook her; because obviously he would want to know more. She expected it, she had a fictitious background worked out in her mind; but in the mind and on the tongue are different things.

So she put the phone down after Frankie's call and went to roust out the children, still in bed. Then, lightheaded with relief, she hurried to her own room and flung her few clothes into the case. When she got back to the living room—Rosher's living room—the boy was there already dressed and smoking pot, making stubs to leave in the ashtray. He couldn't even have washed, the mucky young pup.

As soon as she could gather them together they left the house, the girl turning off to the right, she and the boy to the left, making for the bus station. The man on watch opposite, with no legal authority to stop them, opted to follow the twosome. They left the town as they arrived, by coach. One for Birmingham, one for Bradford; and the discreet policeman learned that they were booked right through.

The girl Helen. There are people who maintain that all delinquency is a spinoff from poor environment, and they may be right. Certainly her background was not particularly good—her mother was a whore who took her into the pornographic film business before she vanished with a Norwegian sea captain,

144

leaving her in care of her elder sister; another whore who didn't care what the kid got up to or where, so long as she was out from under the feet. But even if the psychologists and allied trades are right, it cannot be denied that some children seem born to embrace depravity with wicked enthusiasm.

Today's task was right along Helen's avenue. The pigs, of course, she hated. Frankie, the handsome, laughing pig-baiter, she adored. She would have done the job willingly, for nothing but the sheer exciting joy of it; and he was paying her. That added to her enthusiasm, she had learned very early the desirability of money.

Demure in her jeans and bright top, then, brassiered modestly now and with her hair tied back into a ponytail, the picture of virgin innocence and pretty as a spring daisy, she presented herself at the vicarage; and when the lady who came in daily answered her ring on the bell, she asked for Mr. Pew. Mr. Pew saw her in his study. As soon as she finished her story, he telephoned the police.

Almost immediately afterwards she asked if she could use the lavatory. He showed her where it was; left her alone to use it; and never saw her again. Nor did the cleaning lady.

It made him feel a bit foolish, when the policeman came; but he passed on her allegation that Detective Sergeant Rosher had interfered with her from the very day he, the Reverend Pew, introduced her to the house at the request of Councillor Mrs. Bagster, and had achieved intercourse with her twice. He had also been pestering her mother, and she believed he smoked something funny, because her brother had a friend who did and he said a stub in Rosher's ashtray was the same.

The policeman left the house thinking here was a rum-do. When he got back to the station he learned that a muffled voice over the telephone just before nine o'clock said that in Rosher's house was a hot television set and money from the raided boutique. Asked to identify itself, the voice rang off.

Jokey Fenton that was, ringing very reluctantly at Frankie's insistence. This call, too, was reported later to Inspector Cruse.

Squarely on the shoulders of the Chief Constable squatted the heaviest, most explosive kind of can, one that could blow his head right off; and standing in the downstairs shop of the condemned building opposite the Southgate Branch of Barclays Bank—central bank in the town—he knew it. Knew it so potently that under a bleak and formidable exterior the gut churned and the bowel—unrelieved as yet this morning, there simply hadn't been time—threatened a melting into water.

Standing beside him at the shop window, but well to the side so that glancing passersby would not be confounded by big men unaccountably staring out from an empty shop, were the Chief Superintendent in charge of the Serious Crimes Squad and his own departmental heads; Chief Superintendent (Percy) Fillimore from CID; and Chief Superintendent (Rolly) Rawlins, Uniform Branch. The Serious Crimes Squad Chief murmured:

"Not too many shoppers about, sir. That's a good thing."

"Yes," the Chief Constable said briefly. Silence returned.

A good thing indeed. Here was his great fear: that somebody now innocently walking about wondering whether to buy fish, the terrible price it is, or look for a bit of cheap offal, would suddenly get shot. Because armed men were out there, mingling with them. Some in shops, examining goods; some—Cruse among them, with the unarmed and not informed Sergeant Rosher by his side—sauntering. Male and female both. In this day of women's emancipation, the WPC is stood into danger as readily as the man. Greater danger, in fact, since she very rarely is issued a gun.

Damn, damn, and damn again, as he had damned since it happened, the call from Frankie telling the whispering man he would not be wanted at the meeting. That little man was to fill in all the details—and, in particular, the pickup location. Plan until then was to be there, hidden. Come among them suddenly, somewhere less peopled than this. Get them as they stooped off-guard to enter the cars, the two shotguns probably unloaded; and if not, impossible to bring into action without high risk of

146

blasting holes in each other. Bundle them in, guns, pickax handles, stocking masks, stolen cars and all; with little risk of bystanders being hurt.

Now, that plan had fallen down. Out there were armed men, waiting; and somewhere, two cars, and villains equipped with shotguns. Bleakly, the Chief Constable stood discreetly hidden from the sidewalk, gazing through the grubby window into a sunlit street. Waiting.

10

One common factor shared by all humanity, within which category may be lumped both villain and copper: the upbeating of the heart, the tingle of adrenaline-charge as the moment for action arrives. When the Securicor van came, at nine forty-five by arrangement with the police (who chose this time as relatively quiet, office people safely inside and shopping not yet in spate), bent little Algy up in his room, the Chief Constable and his cohorts below, the casual saunterers and window-shoppers all shared this common experience. Men gave one shoulder a twitch, to feel the reassuring bulge under the arm; women peered more closely yet at dresses on toffee-nosed plastic models, corner of eye using window reflection to see what was happening behind. And the Chief Superintendent in charge of the Serious Crimes Squad said, quite needlessly:

"Here she comes."

The Chief Constable's reply was no more than a grunt. Nobody else said a word; but the tension from their suddenly stiffened bodies quivered almost palpably in the room.

Any press photographer with an eye beyond the mere headlines would have sold his prostituted soul to be here this morning. There was material about that might in some measure have redeemed his perverted years in the newspaper whore trade.

But to get the full picture he would have needed to be in several places at once. Here, where the bulky men, self-forgotten, stared from relative shadow, grim eyed and rocky-jawed faces front lit, into the street; upstairs, where Algy twitched his eye madly, holding his walkie-talkie in both hands as a squirrel holds nuts; quite unable to utter the first of his words, a wonderful study in terror with all his mind shrieking: run—run—; out in the street, to catch if his genius ran to it the underlying tension sharpening eyes set in elaborately casual faces; in the Securicor van itself, where men not bothering to hide tension sat bolt upright; and round two nearby side street corners, where motorcars stood.

In the one parked toward the top of Jover Street, Frankie saw the van go by and echoed precisely the words of the Serious Crimes Squad Chief, "Here she comes."

Nobody else said anything; except Neddy Seamon, in the driving seat, who murmured low as he worked the clutch like a pianist trying the soft pedal: "Thank Christ for that." Best driver in the business, but like most men of quick mind and instinctive skilled reaction, he hated the waiting. Always had before an event, in his days as a racing driver.

Frankie slipped the shotgun out from his tool bag; broke it, to slide the blanks home; checked the heavy metal cutters; riding high now on his fix of adrenaline. He would have liked a rundown on the way things looked in Southgate—if Algy's timing assessment was a trifle off, could they draw in to wait endless seconds at the curb, inconspicuously; or was parking space close to the bank all taken up?—but a rundown meant talk; and beyond the two chosen words, Frankie, like the police and for the same reasons, had decreed radio silence.

A minute, in times like this, is forever. Two is intolerable. One of the men in the back of the car spoke savagely. "Where the fucking hell is he?"

"Shut up," said Frankie. When it came, the word might be a

149

whisper, so low to be lost under extraneous speaking. He lowered his head, to mask from passersby the walkie-talkie held up now, close to his ear. "Quarry," the set should have said. Superfluously, from his point of view. Here in Jover Street, he had seen the van go by; but Jokey would not see it. Rose Lane was further down, beyond the bank. Come on, come on, his mind said: Let's have it, for God's sake. He couldn't have mucked up the frequencies?

In the other car Jokey and his men, in the bare shop the Chief Constable with his co-workers listened as closely for the word from their radios; but neither this word nor its followup—Mayday, when Algy saw the money coming out of the bank—was ever spoken. In the office above, hit suddenly by the full enormity of what he had done, Algy was spewing his ring up, gibbering now in a wave of absolute terror. Things get around; and retribution in the underworld is swift, and certain, and very ugly. Someone would guess—someone would guess.... I didn't mean to do it to you, fellers—only to Frankie. You know me— I'm mad—I'm mad. I didn't even think about you—only about Frankie.

There was still time, even in this last minute, for Frankie to cry off. That he didn't was due to several factors, one of them adrenaline. It speeds the thinking; but it narrows it. And Frankie's mind—an Irish mind, incapable of caution once the action started—was set on going forward, not back. Then again: Suppose his own set had gone wrong, and Jokey was receiving. Fiasco, for the other car to roar suddenly into Southgate, all alone. Jokey might pull the job on his own—but Frankie's image would never live it down, if he skulked here in a side street or was fleeing while the hit happened. All his prestige hung here—and what of the cut? The lads with Jokey—Jokey himself—they wouldn't take kindly to equal shares for the men who spent the crucial time tooling away down side streets.

On the other hand, Jokey might be in the same position, stuck with a silent radio. He, too, would not know whether to go forward or back off. It could be his, Frankie's, car that shot out alone into Southgate.

Well, better that than the other. Much better. If *he* pulled it off on his own, the finger pointed to the other car. His own reputation as a leader of infinite dash and humor (men called him Mad Frankie, and said it with admiring laughter on the lips), far from being ruined would blaze right over the moon.

All this, in capsule form, shot through his mind as he listened to the silent radio; until with sudden decision he shoved it aside and snapped: "Let's go."

It says much for his prestige that nobody demurred. Or perhaps it points more to the effect of adrenaline and the way it concentrates thinking to the action ahead. Neddy Seamon, reaching already for the ignition key before his leader finished speaking, did with hands and feet the things that have to be done. The car slid forward while the occupants removed their headwear, revealing beneath little skullcaps made from the tights or stocking; rolled the nylon down over faces, creating monsters with squashed noses and taut skin, and mouths that sucked unlipped hollows when used for breathing. As the car came up to the Southgate corner, Neddy put his right foot down.

Detective Sergeant Rosher was not really baffled. Puzzled, rather, when instead of driving on through Southgate toward Hipwell Green, Cruse stopped the car and led him to a deserted shop, where the Chief Constable stood with a quantity of upper brass and eyed him with a hard eye, saying not a word to him. Saying only, to young Cruse: "Ah, Alec. Carry on."

Seasoned policeman that he was, the setup was immediately plain. Some bastard was going to hit Barclays. To his eye, the profession of some of those saunterers out there was very obvious. So wind had come, and the bastard when he arrived was in for a surprise. What puzzled the sergeant was: Why had he been told he was on his way to a break-and-enter at Hipwell Green, and personally collected to be brought here? Didn't make sense. Nor did the way young Cruse was covertly watching him as they joined the sauntering company. Almost embarrassed about it, he looked. Bloody funny business.

When the Securicor vehicle came into the street he did not

need Cruse's muttered "This is it" to tell him that indeed it was. All along the pavements close to the bank, very unobtrusively the saunterers were murmuring to people, quietly getting them into shops, according to orders, out of a possible line of fire. The bastards have got guns, then, he thought; and turned to help Cruse persuade an old lady who didn't want to go there that Sainsbury's was a good place to be, and keep away from the window.

Then the cars roared into the street.

By one of those quirks of unfathomable fate, the timing was perfect. Even more perfect, perhaps, than if Algy had given the signal. As the car from Jover Street turned into Southgate, so did the one out of Rose Lane. Jokey had come to the same conclusion that his Chief had reached. To go back, if the other car went forward, was to lose face forever. To go forward if the other went back—to pull the job alone—that way lay high kudos; and possibly, Frankie weakened by it, ultimate leadership.

Whether they were glad to see each other as their respective cars straightened into Southgate or whether the newly rooted thought of lone glory evaporated in a certain disappointment is a moot point. Probably nobody in the cars felt anything much beyond the kick of blood, concentrated as they were entirely upon the Securicor van standing outside the bank, two guards by the open rear doors, two men in the cab.

Other things were there to see; but almost certainly, they failed to register two huge pantechnicons rumbling out from the side streets a block beyond the ones where they themselves had waited, and a sudden flux of blue serge as policemen came out of them, jumping from the tailboards while they were still on the move. They came to rest, these big, lumbering vehicles, right across the road; and the police formed a chain—those who were not racing to shepherd people into shops. From the bottom ends of the streets, where their cars had waited, police cars moved up fast now toward Southgate, to block the only other escape routes.

152

But the lads were totally concentrated. And yes—the timing was perfect. One car squealed to a halt pointing up Southgate, the other pointing down. Takeoff in different directions, to confuse; rendezvous fixed. Men in overalls with stocking masks and pickax handles piled out, and two with sawed-down shotguns and heavy metal cutters; exactly as the money came out through the bank doors. And a whistle blew. A good old-fashioned police whistle such as is rarely heard nowadays, cutting through the air.

Four men raced toward the cab and the guards, pickax handles uplifting; the other two made straight for the two men emerging with the money, in small cases attached by chains to their wrists. And Detective Inspector Cruse turned; as all those idle saunterers turned, suddenly purposeful, to close in. "Come on," he snapped. But Sergeant Rosher needed no urging. Fault him where you will, the chips down, he'd fight rhinoceros, with his bare hands.

It was all very swift, and very confused. No way the six attackers could have known the men in the van cab, the two guards, the two men with the money were all policemen, and that in those cases was cut-up paper only. So the four characters with raised pickax handles, when they rushed up and found themselves facing the barrels of Webley .38's, stopped with a jerk and surrendered from pure shock. If Frankie and Jokey had done the same, the matter would have ended there and then.

Unfortunately, they didn't. Neither realized what was happening, neither heard the whistle, saw the men with guns closing in, or heard the clatter of dropped pickax handles as their mates thrust both hands into the air. All these things were happening simultaneously while they raced for the men with the money; and found pointing at them those wicked, gleaming barrels; heard one of the men shout: "Hold it! Hold it there!"

O Christ! thought Frankie. O Christ—O Christ!

He turned somehow, to head for the cars standing ready, with their engines running.

Nobody shot at him. Why should they? There was no way out.

Orders were as always: Shoot only if the villain fires first; and no villain had fired yet. Frankie still held his shotgun, true; but he showed no intention of using it. The half-dozen guns trained on him would have cut him down anyway before he pulled the trigger, had he tried; because, orders not withstanding, coppers are human, and a man gets a twitchy finger with a shotgun on the rampage.

Jokey it was who upset the pattern of orderly apprehension and arrest. Deadly little man. On the run he leveled his shotgun and fired. Harmlessly, it was loaded with blanks. Perhaps he thought to create diversion, to spread fear. Perhaps it was the instinctive reaction of a deadly little man. With hardly time to be surprised even that he was still alive the policeman fired once. The shot went wide, straight in through the open window of the car in which Neddy Seamon, aware of the roadblock and sobbing with fear, sat with the engine revved up and roaring. It took him in the upper arm as Jokey flung his knife and staggered when the Webley barked again, weaved three more steps of his run before he fell, dead at the feet of the swaying policeman; who dropped his gun and gripped with both hands the hilt of the knife protruding from his chest; and fell across the enemy body, a look of surprise on his face. In the shop, gripping the window ledge with knuckles that showed white, the Chief Constable said over and over again: "Bastard—bastard—bastard—"

Neddy Seamon was no coward. A coward racing driver is a contradiction in terms. But he was in a state of utter confusion and shock, because only he and Bobby Terriss, driving the other car, could see the roadblock and the men with the guns. Hit, he tumbled out of the car crying: "I'm shot—oh, Christ—I'm fucking shot—"; and over his body, in through the open door went Frankie. The car, bucketing away, added to Neddy's problem by running over his legs.

Up in the dusty office, mad Algy Kadowski babbled with his hands over his face, all the fingers wet with tears: "Our Father which art in Heaven...."

Detective Inspector Cruse and Detective Sergeant Rosher, the former with gun in hand, were the nearest policemen to the car as it took off in a shriek of rubber. Both sprang together; and there should be heavy penalties for those who permit their dogs to foul the public footpath. Cruse slipped and went down, the shrieking wheels narrowly missing his head, his gun firing harmlessly into the air; but Rosher stuck, and was borne away on the bonnet; scrabbling for finger-grip, impelled there by pure instinctive reaction and without any desire to be a hero; saying aloud—the vocabulary of action is very limited—: "Fuck it—fuck it—fuck it—fuck it—"

At the wheel, Frankie found himself driving blind, all his forward vision blocked by the big, gorilla-shaped body of a one-time Police All-England Boxing Champion. Sobbing curses, he twisted the wheel this way and that, foot down hard and the powerful car leaping forward, tires screaming from the weaving as he tried to get rid of the body; crying: "Get off, you cunt—get off—get off—" Even a fastidious man brought up in a Catholic home can be weaned from vocal virtue, given sufficient temptation.

He did not see the men, in and out of uniform, who ran into the road waving arms, and jumped aside as the car bore down upon them. All he could see was the body—not even the face—and he couldn't get rid of it.

He could not see how the gorilla on the bonnet had almost enfolded himself across the windscreen, clinging with fingertips in the rain guttering when the centrifugal force slid him one way, bracing knees and toe-caps against the swing of the car as it tugged him the other. He did not see the blue policemen lined across the road in front of the pantechnicon scatter; it is doubtful if he felt the car hit. Moving fast now—the advertising matter claims 60 mph in just a few seconds—smack it went, straight into the great, slab-sided wagon; as Frankie grabbed with one hand at the shotgun slung on the seat beside him, to bring it to bear on Rosher.

Mark of utter panic, that he should do that? Rosher, belly and chest to the windscreen, was looking in at him now with eyes

155

jutting out of his big face like doorknobs, mouth rounded into a comical O. A gun loaded with blanks, with laminated glass between won't blast a man off a car bonnet. On the contrary, the flame is more likely to bounce back, to the detriment of the man inside. Perhaps Frankie didn't intend to fire, perhaps he thought the very look of that gun would persuade the body that it ought to go. But the car hit and the thing went off.

Doubtful, whether Frankie ever knew that the flame shot across his face, searing his eyes out as he smashed forward across the steering wheel. Doubtful if he ever felt the smash of his head against the windscreen, or knew of the glass shattering and the flying sliver that slashed across his throat, so that he lay unconscious and dying with the deep life pumping from the severed jugular vein almost before Rosher, catapulted from the crumpling bonnet, thumped into the wagon's side and fell, bouncing sideways into the road; and lay still.

11

Frankie was dead. Jokey was dead. Detective Constable Basil St. John Armitage, twenty-five, married with two children, was dead. Detective Sergeant Rosher had been carted off to the hospital, condition report not yet in. The smashed car, clotted inside with blood, had been towed to the police compound, the damaged removal truck had limped away, and a quantity of shattered glass lay in a glittering greenish pile, swept into the gutter. Life in Southgate was returning to normal, traffic flow as usual. And now the Chief Constable sat grim faced at his desk, his phone disconnected from the station switchboard, which buzzed madly and incessantly as the press fell wolfishly upon the story. Down there, the WPC on duty read again and again through a hastily prepared official handout.

The chief among all chief constables—fussy, dapper little person from the city who ruled even this man, and all the chiefs in the towns of the county similarly situated, center of a cluster of lesser towns and villages—had been driven in, had spoken his qualified approval of the job's handling, had tut-tutted his concern over the death of a policeman and the necessary gun-play that eliminated two other lives, and driven out. The various

157

brass engaged had departed, to make reports and take up other more mundane tasks set aside while Frankie was dealt with. In the office now were three men only: the Chief Constable himself; Detective Inspector Cruse; and Detective Inspector John Barclay. The Chief was speaking.

"So that's it. Just the odds and ends to clear up. And the other matter, of course. Alec—get up to see Mrs. Bagster, will you?"

"Now, sir?" Cruse, too, spoke out of a mouth set harder than usual in a grim face. Beside him Inspector Barclay stood in silence, equally stony eyed. Policemen do not enjoy bloodletting, and the death of a colleague spreads anger and a sort of tense, sad edginess over an entire force. And, of course, after extreme tension comes the emotional letdown.

"Now. Take the transcript with you. If you don't get the right answers, bring her in."

"Right." He'd be bringing her in, no doubt about that. Nothing connected her with the bank raid; but anybody so obviously *persona grata* with the late Mad Frankie Daly had to be looked at, very closely.

"John," the Chief Constable said, "I want you to go over Rosher's house. Here's the list of things said to be in there." He pushed within Barclay's reach a typed sheet of paper.

The inspector picked it up. "Warrant, sir?" he asked.

"Not necessary—I want this cleared up now." Warrants come by application to a magistrate. A Chief Constable, or any high-ranking brass, can eliminate delay by authorizing search if circumstances call for it and he is prepared to shoulder the can.

"Uh-huh," said Inspector Barclay; and turned with Cruse to leave as the intercom buzzed. The Chief Constable flicked the switch; listened to a report just come in as the door closed behind them.

Police stationed behind the condemned building, as behind all the buildings along Southgate, had observed the man Algernon Kadowski going in, and let him pass without showing themselves, according to orders. When he failed to emerge after the incident, having received their recall, they entered the building.

The little man knelt in the middle of a first floor office, babbling prayers and weeping with the light of glory in his face, apparently undergoing an attack of religious hysteria. He had been removed by police car to the psychiatric unit of the hospital of St. John, calling upon the officers to repent.

Councillor Mrs. Bagster guessed that the police would be coming, but she had not expected that it would be so soon. Local politicians concerned enough to keep an ear on happenings within their sphere of influence normally listen to the local BBC radio station. Mrs. Bagster always switched on at one o'clock, to hear the lunchtime news bulletin. Today, it told her of the raid. Made the main feature out of it and the deaths; as would all the national stations, the TV networks, and the hungry newspapers, their men with microphones and cameras and notebooks already rushing here to cook up a meal out of corpses for a slavering public almost unfed since last week, when a man with a butcher's knife dismembered his wife and four children in a basement flat at Pimlico.

Her first reaction as the name Frank Daly sprang out at her was pure shock; followed immediately by a wave of relief. He was dead—oh, thank you, God—he was dead, the evil, sweet-speaking man was dead. So were others—the equally evil Joseph Fenton—and a policeman—but in that first upsurge of relief, she hardly heard their names. When the full implications came to her as mind caught up with emotion, she thought: This is going to be all over the headlines—all over the country. Anything connected with Daly is going to be big news—and you are connected with Daly—they will investigate all his affairs—

The police, they would scrutinize everything—his books, his papers, his photographs. . . . They would pry, with the eyes of the world upon them, they would leave no stone unturned. This phrase actually went through her mind. Politicians by nature think in cliché.

In all the course of her life she had never been a hard drinker; but of late she spent a good deal of time with the whisky bottle. Her friends, council colleagues, boutique staffs were beginning to whisper, to raise eyebrows at one another when she spoke, and the consonents slurred a little. But not her husband, he didn't notice. Too wrapped up in grocery and golf to notice anything she did, so long as he was fed and had clean underwear. Well, let there be justice: Marriage to a bolster-bosomed lesbian lady brings certain problems. Grocering and golf are as good a means to survival as any.

She went to the bottle now. Had been with it for an hour when Detective Inspector Cruse arrived, fuddling the terror, unable to decide what Frankie's death had done to her. Did it liberate her—perhaps his photographs were kept in a secret, undiscoverable place—or did it mean the end, in a spectacular blaze of perfervid headlines? Nothing criminal in the photographs, unless the younger girl was in fact underage, but the mere linking of her with that kind of sex was the finish. The police would not publish them, but even if, politically and socially ruined, she brazened it out (without her husband—he'd be off like a rabbit) in the town—how could she ever again look into the eye of a policeman, from Chief Constable down? Always, she would see in imagination contempt in the educated man, a snigger hidden under the impassive features of the lowly rank. They would all have seen them—they'd hand them round at the station, for a good laugh. The imagination, in times of such stress, tends to run amuk. And quite apart from the sex angle—the picture linked her firmly with the criminal element led by Frankie Daly. Hers would be headlines topping even his, turning sensation into Story of the Year.

Sitting alone in her lovely drawing room with the bottle beside her on a fine antique occasional table, she heard the car arrive and the chiming note of the front door bell, and her overwrought mind said at once: Oh, my God—they're here. But she stayed sitting upright in her chair, the world made wavy by whisky; until the daily lady who cleaned and doubled up with duty, while she was here, as maid, appeared and said:

"It's two policemen, Mrs. Bagster. They want to see you."

Her whisky-burdened stomach gave a great lurch, even

though she had known who it would be. "What policemen, Mrs. Neal?" she asked, pulling on the extreme dignity of the unsober.

"One in a suit, says his name's Inspector Cruse. The other one's got a uniform. I don't know what his name is." A very plain, middle-aged woman, this, with an ulcerated leg. No pretty living-in maid here. Mrs. Neal was Councillor Bagster's insurance against her own sexual proclivities.

"Show them in." The councillor waved a kingly hand.

"Yes, madam," said Mrs. Neal; and as she went back to the front door, she thought: pissed again.

When she brought the policemen in, Mrs. Bagster was standing over by the sideboard, having just smuggled the bottle into it, out of sight. The key to the cupboard was still in her hand and her glass stood half filled where she had been sitting. Inspector Cruse noted it all. He said:

"Good afternoon, madam."

"Good afternoon." The same one who came before. But this time looking not quite so young, without his boyish smile. Mrs. Neal was hovering. "Thank you, Mrs. Neal," the lady said. "That will be all."

"Yes, madam," said Mrs. Neal, and exited with a slight sniff. Nobody need think she was agog. Mind you, it might be nothing. Something to do with them delinquents, or the police ball. Or unmarried mothers. Not that the old bat did much in that line these days, the cheeky little buggers just went out to work and kept 'em.

The young policeman had lost more than his boyish smile. All the deference was gone from his manner and his eyes were a cold slate gray. Last time he was here they were little boy blue. As soon as Mrs. Neal was gone, without waiting for invitation to proceed he said:

"I think you know why I am back, madam."

"Er—," said Councillor Mrs. Bagster. "Er—"

"You told me you had no knowledge of Frank Daly."

"I—er—" O God. "I—er—yes. I remembered afterwards—I have met him—"

"Rather more than met him, madam, I would suggest." One

161

thing he had not lost: the rather archaic phraseology. Snap in the voice and sudden accidental overalliteration did not altogether destroy it.

"I—er—I have met him."

"We believe you know him well, madam. We believe you know him very well."

She read contempt into his eyes and into the carefully stolid face of the constable standing beside him. Truth is, the snapping hostility in Cruse's manner was built upon upset and strain. He held no particular brief for this woman, she must be bent; but at any normal time he would have approached less brusquely.

She was not to know his upset. One thing only was on her mind, and the subject's fear confers upon a visiting policeman the attributes of avenging God. She read contempt into his slate-gray eyes and thought: They've got them. They're poring over them now, passing them from hand to hand at the station. The Chief Constable—these two—they'll all have seen them. "I—no," she said. "Not—well. I—met him. Once. Or twice."

"More than that, madam." The young man was drawing a paper from his pocket. "Would you care for me to refresh your memory? I have here a transcript of your telephone call immediately after my previous visit."

She did not ask how such a transcript came into existence. Could not even remember, in her fear and whisky-fuddle, what she said to Frankie in the course of the call. What did it matter, anyway? She stared back now into the cold eyes, remustering something of dignity. "Are you here to arrest me?"

"No, madam. Not to arrest you. But I must ask you to accompany me to the station. There are matters that would appear to merit investigation."

The half-drunken dignity grew visibly, almost comically. Definitely comic, this tweed-clad square lady with the bolster bosom, drawn up stiffly to full height like mother-in-law in an old British upper-bracket stage farce, but not entirely steady on big, brogued feet. Worth a laugh; except for the glistening gray sweat of fear on the suddenly flabbing skin, the sheen of fear in the fine eyes. "What matters?" the lady said.

162

"I think you know, madam." The young man's attitude, influenced perhaps by her assumption of dignity, had hardened into curt-voiced authority. All the power of the law stood behind him and he spoke the unforgiving weight of it. "We have reason to believe that your relationship with Frank Daly and his affairs is more intimate than you intended us to think." Reason to believe. Not proof. Nothing is proof, until proven in a court of law.

His choice of words was not deliberate; it was purely the result of extemporization in speech. He might have phrased it in any one of half a dozen different ways; but he said relationship—affairs—intimate—and in people with knowledge of court phraseology and Sunday-paper euphemism who have sexual abberation on the mind, these words hit nerves. They confirmed in Councillor Mrs. Bagster the belief that they knew it all—they had the photographs, they had arrested the people planted in the sergeant's house—they knew everything.

Suddenly she felt herself completely sober, for the first time in many days. There was true dignity in her manner now, as she said: "Very well. Am I permitted to leave a note for my husband? He will be home soon."

The young policeman nodded. She walked, quite steadily, over her rich carpet and through into her husband's quiet, paneled study; closed the door behind her and crossed into the attached greenhouse, where the jobbing gardener kept his tools. From a shelf she took a bottle, an ordinary lemonade bottle with a piece of paper stuck over the original label, lettered in the gardener's crabby hand, smeared by his earthy fingers: DANGEROUS. Quickly, because the policeman might be following right behind her, she drew the cork and tilted the bottle against her lips. The basic weed-killing ingredient was Paraquat.

On the Chief Constable's desk stood an ashtray from Rosher's house, containing ash and the stubs of two thin, self-rolled cigarettes; and a slim packet of banknotes found in Rosher's attic, numbers checked against the list of notes stolen from the dead Mrs. Bagster's boutique and found to match. Silent in the sunny office, Detective Inspectors John Barclay and Alec Cruse watched while their grim-faced chief picked up one of the stubs—he had done it several times, almost unconsciously after the first check, body automatically occupying itself while the mind went its own way—and sniffed at it.

No doubt as to what it was. Clinging to it still was the characteristic odor. He put it back into the ashtray, careful not to touch the smooth surface of the tray itself upon which a plethora of fingerprints showed, dusted up by the men from Forensic; picked up the little bundle of notes; put them down again. Said to the two silent men:

"Well?"

For a second neither replied, each deferring, perhaps, to the other. Then Inspector Barclay spoke, very shortly. "Plant."

"You think so?" Marble-hard eyes watched the long-service man's nod; moved on to young Cruse. The steel bark addressed him coldly. "What about you?"

Alec Cruse knew well enough the reason for this sudden withdrawal of favor. It added to the general upset of this terrible, terrible day. Why, for Christ's sake, did he let her out of his sight? Apart from the appalling horror of her agonized end—he had followed her in after a little time elapsed, and she writhed to death before the ambulance arrived—here was a big black mark against him, more than nullifying any kudos he may have earned for his part in the Frankie Daly affair. He had let a prominent local politician go off alone, to drink Paraquat. The press would enjoy it, all nicely tied in with the Daly sensation. Paraquat was always good news. He'd come very badly out of the enquiry—which the Old Man would conduct, with his marble eye.

How the hell had he let her do it? Tired, yes—exhausted, with lost sleep and emotional reaction after the morning caper; but tiredness, exhaustion, mental depression, and preoccupation with ugly death come to three men, one a colleague—none of it counts as excuse when a policeman blunders. Certainly, this hard man brooked no excuse, for any action that reflected badly upon the efficiency and general conduct of his force.

164

Poor old cow. Oh, poor old woman. What a terrible way to go. And she wasn't in all that deeply.

Or was she? We'll find out more, no doubt, when Daly's affairs are gone into properly.

"I think it's a plant, sir," he said. "The things and the people both."

"Obviously." The Chief snapped hard, glad of a chance to hammer home his disfavor. If the articles were a plant, the people had to be. Definitely. The whole thing sang of plant. Would any policeman seasoned and wily as Rosher fill up his house with hot marked money and a stolen television set, and sit in it frigging about with a little girl, touching up her mother and smoking pot in the intervals? Of course it was a bloody plant.

So who did it help, their knowing it? Certainly not him. The presence of the stuff in Rosher's house, the vanished child's allegations—there had to be an enquiry. At bottom of the whole messy pack, the Chief smelled a joker. Oh, yes—the bent would have a field day. But *he* wasn't laughing. No humor in the gaze fixed upon Cruse. Another enquiry, involving the death of next year's mayor and this bloody young fool. Basilisk eyed, he waited for the fool to say more.

It was Inspector John Barclay who broke up the silence. "The boy's known, sir. Bradford will have him in no time. We'll soon gather the other two in."

True, most likely. The lad would never stand up to the grilling he would undoubtedly receive. He would grass, especially when he knew that Frankie, at whose instigation these people seemed to have been planted, was dead and beyond the sphere in which he could exact retribution. But the thought afforded no comfort. He grunted; picked up the money and put it down again; brooded a moment; and then said:

"All right, John—thank you. Better get back to work."

"Sir," said Inspector Barclay, and prepared to leave. The Chief addressed Cruse.

"You'd better come with me. Hospital, to see Rosher."

"Is he all right, sir?" the young man asked. Last time he saw

165

Rosher the man was on a stretcher, asking out of semiconscious fog for information regarding the whereabouts of his black hat—the hat that had been prized from his bentover ears, having at last proved its intrinsic worth by cushioning impact when skull met pantechnicon. Inspector Barclay paused on his way out, to hear the reply.

"Conscious. Bust up a bit, but conscious." The Chief arose from his swivel chair, to gather his own gray fedora from its peg.

Detective Sergeant Rosher lay bandaged and plastered in his hospital bed, accepting with philosophic stoicism the discomfort of one broken leg trussed up in a sling, one broken arm in another, one dented skull, one badly battered eye, and a few ribs stove in. Physical injury never bothered him very deeply. He dealt with it and took it in fun, during his boxer days, and it is an integral part of a policeman's work, the taking and giving of pain, the witnessing of inflicted injuries. Long familiarity plus a tough durability bred into that gorilla body enabled him to treat pain with contempt, even to find in it spur to greater physical endeavor, as when he came off the floor to score a knockout. He lived well with pain; so long as it confined itself to the physical. Against mental agony, he was less well equipped.

But today he had no mental pain. One of the properties of action and pain resulting from action, to the active man, is that it clears the mind wonderfully. He lay in bed with a bubble inside him of actual happiness.

He had returned to full consciousness while they were strapping and plastering. His first coherent utterance had been a request that somebody telephone his house, to tell his housekeeper where he was and to ask that she bring in his own pajamas and dressing gown, to replace the flannel hospital issue into which they had manipulated him while his wits wandered.

No answer to the call, they said. Shopping, no doubt, he told himself, and asked that they keep trying at intervals, until she returned. The young black nurse with the very white smile plumped up his pillows as nurses feel impelled to do in obedience to itching vocation and went away, leaving him to his thinking; in which Frankie Daly and the events that put him here—he knew nothing of Detective Constable Armitage's death—had no part.

He thought about her. Shopping, as at this moment; basket on arm, concentrated on buying the meat, the vegetables, all things necessary for the next wonderful meal. Sitting plump and demure on his settee, watching television with him, eating delicately when they shared supper. Occupying the seat beside him in the car while he drove through country beautiful as he had never seen it before; walking with him beside a still lake, drinking with him at a rough bench outside an old pub. The white sweet upper swell of her breasts, when she leaned over his coffee table.

She would be here, soon. She would appear through that door there, the one way into this single-bedded annex stuck onto the main ward, bringing his pajamas and other gear. Lovely and—worried? Upset—so that he would have to comfort her, tell her not to fret, this was nothing compared to what a nut called Charlie Higgins did to him with an ax, when he ran amuck in 1963.

Perhaps he would—speak—to her. Not necessarily this time, if she was upset. But she would be coming again.

Divorce is not difficult to acquire, these days. Not even expensive, really. People remarry. He drifted into sleep. Leg in a sling, arm in another, ribs swathed in strapping, head in a bandage skullcap that covered one eye, he closed his good eye into contented slumber. His last thought was: We may even find I'm a hero.

A voice called him back. A steel-edged voice, barking his name. "Rosher! Rosher!" Just his name, repeating itself into his dream. He opened the one working eye. Beside his bed stood two big men, the Chief Constable and young Cruse. Detective Constable Cruse—Detective Sergeant Cruse—Detective Inspector Cruse, who moved into his old office. In the background hovered the pretty black nurse, perturbed because she told the men he was asleep and the older one barked: "Wake him up, then—

wake him up," and marched straight in, to do it himself.

Seeing the eye open, the Chief Constable glanced briefly at the nurse. "That will be all, miss. Thank you." She fluttered a moment and went. The stern man had an iron face. He turned it back to Rosher. "Well, Sergeant," he said.

"Ah," said Rosher, his mind stiffened automatically into its normal resentment against this man who, having bust him, had ground him with fresh humiliation every day since.

The Chief Constable did not ask after his health—he knew the state of it anyway, from the hospital report—or express sympathy. He did not commend Rosher for what had been, in truth, a courageous act. There would be no citation, no police medal on his recommendation. He moved straight in.

"I have to tell you that complaint has been laid against you alleging offenses against a minor."

"What?" said Sergeant Rosher, unable to believe his ears, both of which stuck out hairy and unimpeded beneath his white skullcap. "What?"

"The child appears to have absconded, together with two other people who have been living in your house, ostensibly her mother and brother. The woman is known to have criminal connections, particularly with Frank Daly. The boy—"

Rosher scarcely heard the rest, as the iron voice went on to detail the articles found in his house. The lovely, cuddly rainbow-tinted balloon burst in his soul's face, shatteringly. He had been conned—framed—destroyed—. And even now, above the stark recognition that this was it, his ultimate ending, the voice of his soul cried in shock: She's not coming. Never. Never again. She's not coming.

O Christ—what a fool. What a fool—fool—fool.

". . . These matters will be subjected to thorough investigation," the Chief Constable was saying. "In the meantime, I have no alternative but to suspend you, as of today. It is our present belief that the *cannabis* and stolen property were introduced into your house without your knowledge, by the people concerned or their associates. If this proves to be the case, whatever

168

charges are brought against you will be purely a matter of internal discipline." He paused, as if he expected that Rosher would respond, perhaps eagerly, to this proffered chance to claim foolishness in preference to knavery, and so keep everything in the family. When no such response came, he added: "I shall have to institute a full enquiry, of course."

Now Rosher spoke, in a voice hoarse and hardly recognizable as his own. But a last defiance was in it, and in the one glittering, hard eye. "Don't bother," he said. "You can have my resignation." He turned his face away, to the wall. Nothing else would turn.

The Chief Constable stood a moment. Then he said: "Her-r-r-rrumph!" and turned, to leave the room. Young Inspector Cruse, lifted out of preoccupation with his own problems by the sight of the plastered and bandaged, ludicrously sling-supported man in the bed and shaken by the Chief's brutal approach, Rosher's pitifully savage response, hesitated. Thus far, he had not spoken a word. What he said now was sublimely fatuous. He knew it even as it slipped out. He said:

"Keep your pecker up, old son."

Bloody stupid thing to say, he told himself as he followed his master out and along clackingly antiseptic corridors, a young man with worries of his own. Back in his single-bedded annex, Detective Sergeant Rosher lay without moving, staring bleakly out of one good eye at a primrose yellow wall. He did not even know they were gone.